Neverland 2.0

Cora's Tale

by
Lauren M. Flauding

Chapter One

It had been two weeks since Neverland became an amusement park, and by all accounts, it was a huge success. The visitors raved about the fantastical atmosphere and the inventive activities. The money was rolling in and more elements and organisms were being added every day. The inhabitants of Neverland had found new meaning and excitement in their lives. In short, everyone was thrilled that Neverland was open to the public.

Everyone except Cora.

She glared at the other mermaids getting ready for their stupid show and prepared herself for another day of hiding out in the cove behind the waterfalls. Thankfully, Peter had engineered an underwater laptop that kept her busy most of the time. It wasn't as if she interacted much with people anyway, but all of the alone time was becoming rather tedious. Maybe she'd try and play some games with the dolphins today.

She could, of course, hang around their dwelling. It was interesting enough with its glassy spires and jeweled walls. There were numerous rooms and areas for playing and learning, like a small palace with no roof. She could spend her time weaving intricate nets or reprogramming the mechanical fish to do choreographed dances, but Cora didn't like to be reminded of the fact that she lived there. Right now they were all in the common room, which was an area where the mermaids spent a lot of their time. Besides being the only place with mirrors, it was also the only room where they could actually talk to each other. It was encased in a large glass dome so that only the bottom half of the room was submerged in water. This was especially helpful when they got tired of signing to each other, or when they didn't want to go to the surface for air.

"Hey Meredith!" Nerissa called out sharply, cutting into Cora's thoughts. "You got in front of me during the second set of jumps yesterday. Make sure you stay out of my way."

The red-tailed mermaid bobbed her head up and down in compliance. "Of course, Nerissa. It won't happen again."

Cora rolled her eyes. She had a feeling Meredith would cut off her own arm if Nerissa asked her to. Cora could never understand the power Nerissa had over the rest of the mermaids. It was as though she were their queen. Cora studied Nerissa as she braided her long blonde hair into several elaborate strands. She was extremely beautiful, with her large blue eyes and porcelain skin, but Cora didn't think that was reason enough for the other girls to worship her.

Cora glanced at the line of mermaids before her. Piper was covering her arms with some neon glitter that clashed horribly with her bright green tail. Catalina was making kissing faces in the mirror. Her dark blue tail blended in with the water so well that she looked like she was just a floating torso. Meredith was watching Nerissa closely and trying to braid her hair in the same way, but was failing spectacularly.

And Isla, the youngest, was staring dreamily at the wall and gliding her gold tail back and forth across the surface of the water. *Perhaps they follow Nerissa because they're all lost,* Cora thought. They were all lonely, out of their element, confused, insecure. Nerissa was lost too, she was just much better at hiding it.

"You can stare all you want, but you'll never be me," Nerissa said smugly, slapping her pink tail against the water so that it splashed in Cora's face.

Cora blinked the water out of her eyes and scowled at Nerissa. "I consider that a massive blessing. I don't know how I'd survive with all that empty space in my brain."

The other girls gasped and Nerissa flushed with anger.

"If I wasn't worried about ruining my hair, I'd strangle you."

Cora snorted. "Once again, I'm saved by your vanity."

Nerissa charged forward, but Piper and Catalina held her back.

"She's not worth it," Piper said. "Save your energy for your fans."

Nerissa took a deep breath and shook off the other mermaids. "You're right, Piper. I have an adoring public, and she has no one."

Cora shrugged and turned away. She wasn't going to be offended by what she already knew was the truth.

"Come on, girls, it's time to go." Nerissa led the way as they prepared to swim out of the gate at the bottom of the room. But before she dove underwater, she looked back at Cora. "Have fun being a loser."

"Have fun being a joke," Cora shot back.

Nerissa screeched and grabbed a hairbrush, hurling it at Cora's head. Cora flipped her tail up and smacked the hairbrush back at Nerissa, hitting her in the shoulder. Nerissa seethed for a few moments, then signed something at Cora that was too foul to say aloud and disappeared beneath the water. The other mermaids gave Cora nasty looks and followed Nerissa out.

Cora sighed, glad that they were finally gone. She could already feel the space becoming less toxic. But before she could begin gathering the things she needed for the day, the water stirred and Isla emerged into the room again. The young mermaid gave Cora a shy smile.

"I left my necklace," she explained, reaching past Cora for a small silver locket. She started to leave, but then turned back and gave Cora an almost apologetic look. "You should be in the show with us."

Cora's eyebrows shot up. "Uh, no thank you. I'd rather not flail around in front of hundreds of strangers. Plus, I don't think I'm very welcome."

Isla bit her lip. "But Slightly thinks it would be more dynamic if all the mermaids performed."

Cora groaned. She had a lot of things she wanted to say to Slightly, who had decided to commercialize Neverland without even considering how it would affect everyone.

"Well, you can tell *Slightly* that if he wants more mermaids, he can put on a tail and some sea shells and dance around himself. I'm sure he'd love the attention."

Isla giggled. "He'd look ridiculous!"

Cora gave Isla a small smile. The auburn-haired girl could only be 14 or 15 years old, and even then she was small for her age. Isla was still definitely loyal to Nerissa, but she was the only mermaid who had ever attempted to be nice to her.

"Come on, Cora, it'd be fun!" Isla continued. "The kids love us, and we always talk to the fans afterwards. Plus, there are always a few teenage boys there, and they are so cute!"

Cora quirked an eyebrow. "They'll run away screaming when they find out your tail isn't a costume."

Isla frowned. "What do you mean?"

Cora sighed. "Everybody thinks we're just normal humans who put on fancy tails and swim around. That's what they have at other attractions. I read about it on the Internet."

Isla laughed. "That's crazy! There's no way humans could do the things we do."

"Exactly," Cora said bitterly. "Pretty soon they're going to find out that we're real mermaids."

"That'd be great!" Isla exclaimed. "Then we'd be famous!"

"Yeah, famous for being freaks. Then we'll end up in a circus, or in a museum, or in a research lab. I'd actually prefer that last one."

Isla made a face. "You're really depressing, Cora. Maybe this is why Nerissa doesn't like you." Isla dove down into the water and swam out of the room, her gold tail shimmering until the gate closed.

"I'm not depressing, I'm realistic," Cora murmured to herself. "And it's not just Nerissa who doesn't like me, it's the whole world."

Cora laughed out loud at her overdramatic statements, but then she immediately sobered. She tried not to imagine that the whole world was against her, but when she considered her history and her likely future, it was difficult to think otherwise. The other mermaids seemed to be handling it alright, but she couldn't pretend she was living a fantasy.

She shivered at the memories that haunted her every waking moment. She never knew her parents. She had been in orphanages since her birth. Her childhood hadn't been idyllic, but she had dreams. She was going to travel the world. She wanted to see and experience everything. She would pour over atlases and encyclopedias, planning out which countries and landmarks she would see first.

Then that woman had come. She had said her name was Matilda Carnivera, but the others had called her the Crocodile. Cora had just turned nine years old and she had been so excited. She thought she was going to be adopted. She thought she was going to have her chance to escape from the confines of all the orphanages. But the woman had taken her straight to a frightening, sterile facility. Then there were the days and weeks and months of surgeries, pills, medicines, experiments, and nightmares. Days where she struggled to breathe and nights where she felt like her bones were on fire. She would wake up in a haze and feel her body changing, only to lose consciousness again minutes later.

After almost a year, Cora awoke to find herself at the bottom of the lagoon in Neverland. She could see and breathe underwater, she could swim incredibly fast, she could sense something swimming in the water a kilometer away, and in the place of her legs was a shiny purple tail. She had been thrilled for about two hours. She had tested out her abilities and seen some of the most beautiful fish she'd ever imagined. But once she had explored all the exotic sea life and the underwater structures and the entirety of the lagoon, she began to understand the limits of her new world. She was trapped in a massive fish tank.

Cora had met the other kids in Neverland, but they had always been busy creating things and didn't seem interested in befriending her at all. Then other mermaids were brought in, and Cora had thought she might have some camaraderie, but none of them saw the dark side of their situation like she did. They seemed completely content to be mermaids and do the same things day after day. So there was a division. It was constantly her against them, and so far she hadn't had much luck persuading any of them that being half fish wasn't a dream come true.

And now Neverland was open to the public, and the mermaids had put themselves on display. Cora was terrified about what would happen when people found out what they really were. She pushed herself up from the gel pad she was sitting on and gazed at her reflection in the mirror. Her sad grey eyes stared back at her, revealing how lonely she really was. Her curly black hair cascaded down her shoulders and often got tangled in the straps of her sea shells. Cora hated the matching shells that covered her chest, they were so archaic and cliche. But they were functional for living underwater, and it'd be so embarrassing to ask Peter or one of the other boys to develop a more comfortable bra. Cora looked down at her stomach, at the area below her belly button where her skin transitioned into her dark purple tail. The pattern of the luminous scales was always changing, and the effect could be quite hypnotic, but Cora found the more she stared at it, the more bitter she became.

Cora sighed and glanced at herself in the mirror again. Some might consider her beautiful, but she was afraid that when people looked at her, they would just see what she saw. A science experiment.

Chapter Two

"Hey Jack, it looks like some kids are messing around on the east side of the lagoon. Could you check that out?"

"Sure Tink. I'm headed there right now."

Jack Baker adjusted his earpiece and took a deep breath as he navigated his way through the forest. He had been working as a security guard in Neverland for almost a week now, but he still wasn't used to his new job. Security work had a lot of similarities with police work, but Neverland and its systems were a lot to handle.

Some of his former colleagues thought he was crazy for changing careers. After he had brought in James Hook he was offered an impressive promotion, but he didn't really feel that he deserved it. After all, Hook had basically turned himself in. The wanted criminal had appeared outside of the mental institution just as Jack was being discharged, and all Jack had to do was walk him to the police station. On top of all that, Jack had grown disenchanted with police work. It wasn't as fulfilling as he imagined it would be. Becoming a security guard at an amusement park was definitely a step down, but Jack had his reasons. For one, he was mesmerized with Neverland. He had thought it was magical back when it wasn't functioning, so now with everything fixed and optimized for the public, it was just about the most magnificent place he'd ever encountered. And then, of course, there was *her*.

Jack was a little ashamed to admit to himself that his main motive for taking a job in Neverland was to find out more about that mermaid who had saved all of their lives when they were searching for the treasure. All he knew about her was that she was incredibly fast and agile in the water, and that she had one nasty backswing on that purple tail of hers. Oh yeah, and she was drop dead gorgeous. He had spent many nights wondering about her, wondering how she became a mermaid, if that's what she really was, wondering where she lived and how she slept, wondering if she was even human, wondering what she did with her time when she wasn't saving people's lives. He knew it was a little bit ridiculous. Most young men didn't fantasize about girls who lived in the water, especially since their interaction had been short and rather hostile. Memories of her knocking him out with her tail shouldn't make him smile, and yet, here he was. Perhaps he had gone a little crazy.

However, he hadn't seen her in all the time he'd been working in Neverland. He'd seen the other mermaids in their show and chatting with the visitors. They were all beautiful, although they seemed a little vapid. But there was no sign of the dark-haired mermaid with the haunting eyes. He was hoping he'd run into her, but he was afraid that if he didn't see her soon he'd have to do some investigating.

Jack arrived at the beach and immediately saw the perpetrators. Two young boys were standing on a rock and lowering some contraption into the water. When they saw

Jack coming, the boys hastily pulled their device up and tried to conceal it behind the rock.

"What are you boys up to?" Jack asked.

"Nothing," they responded in unison, avoiding Jack's stare.

Jack folded his arms and peered down at them until one of them gave in.

"We were trying to see the mermaids changing into their costumes," he said sheepishly, handing Jack a waterproof camera mounted to a toy motor boat.

Jack chuckled. "Nice try, but that's not allowed," he said, turning the gadget in his hands. "Plus, I believe they've already changed," he added with a wink. "Please don't put anything into the lagoon."

The boys took their camera and sulked away. A minute later, loud, dynamic music sounded from the nearby speakers, signaling the start of the mermaid show. A large crowd had already gathered on the beach, filling up the benches lining the shore. With no more instructions from Tink, Jack walked to the edge of the crowd to watch from the side.

The audience cheered as the five mermaids shot up out of the water. They soared to an unnatural height and then flipped in the air and dove back into the lagoon. They continued on for several minutes, doing impressive maneuvers and intricate sequences. At one point only their tails were out of the water doing synchronized moves, meaning that they were holding their breath for an inordinate amount of time. When they finished, they swam up to the edge of the water to talk to the visitors and take pictures.

Jack watched them interact with the guests. They looked nice enough, but Jack couldn't shake the image of them trying to strangle him to death. He specifically remembered that the one with the blue tail had nearly dragged him to the bottom of the lagoon.

He spotted Slightly sitting on a bench and taking notes nearby and walked over to him. Slightly smiled when he saw him.

"Hey Jack, how's security duty going?"

"It's alright. Nothing too exciting," Jack admitted. "Although I did just catch a couple boys trying to spy on the mermaids changing into their costumes."

Slightly snorted. "Even if they had been able to see the mermaids, I fear they would have been sorely disappointed."

Jack waited for Slightly to elaborate, but he didn't.

"That's a pretty good show they put on," Jack commented, gesturing to the mermaids.

"Yeah," Slightly said with a frown. "Almost too good." He stared out at the lagoon for a moment, and then turned abruptly to Jack. "Did you know that mermaids don't actually exist?"

Jack was a bit surprised at the sudden question. "Um, yes."

Slightly shook his head. "I didn't. I grew up with them here, so I just took them for granted. I always figured that a handful of mermaids had come from someplace else to live here. Now I feel like a twit, and I'm afraid I've created a rather inconvenient situation for them. I might have to tell them to tone down their jumps."

Jack nodded. "That'd probably be a good idea." A few seconds passed before Jack asked a question that had been running through his mind for weeks. He glanced around and lowered his voice. "So then, if they're not actually humans, what are they?"

"That is a mystery," Slightly replied, running his hand through his hair. "They're not normal, that's for sure. I guess I could ask them about it, but I'm not certain they'd even know the answer."

Jack swallowed. "Wow. That's..."

"Weird?"

"Interesting."

"Hm." Slightly closed his notebook and stood up. "Luckily, none of them seem to care that their home is open to the public. Well, except for Cora."

Jack's pulse quickened. *Cora? That must be the dark-haired mermaid,* he thought. *It had to be.*

"Yeah, the one with the purple tail," Jack said, trying to sound nonchalant. "What's her deal anyway?"

Slightly looked sideways at him, a sly smile spreading across his face. He could see right through him. "She left a pretty big impression on you, didn't she?"

Jack exhaled. "I'll say. She sent me to the hospital."

Slightly laughed and clapped his hand on Jack's shoulder. "Out of all the mermaids, Cora is the most level-headed, but she's also the most pessimistic. I don't know if she'll ever be happy."

"Why not?"

Slightly shrugged. "My best guess is that she doesn't want to live in a lagoon for the rest of her life."

Jack scratched his beard thoughtfully, feeling a surge of sympathy for this girl he hardly knew. "Well, do you know where I might find her?" He asked. "I'd like to sort some things out with her and try to be her friend."

Slightly raised his eyebrows. "Ah, come on, Jack. You want to be more than friends. I saw the way you looked at her that day you cut her free from the rock."

Jack sighed. There was no use trying to keep it a secret from Slightly. "Yes," he admitted, "I'd like to be much more than friends."

Jack expected Slightly to laugh, but he just nodded. "Isla told me she usually hangs out behind the waterfalls," Slightly said meaningfully.

Jack smiled. "Thanks."

Slightly started to leave, but Jack stopped him. "Hey, could we keep this between us for now? I don't really want this to turn into a big deal."

"Of course, I understand," Slightly replied. "Being attracted to a girl with a tail is..."

"Weird?"

"Interesting."

*****

The waterfalls were off limits to the public, so Jack didn't really have a reason to go there. He hoped Tink wouldn't give him an assignment when he was so far away from the action. It had been an adjustment getting used to having her voice in his ear all the time.

The first waterfall he checked was inaccessible and the second looked deserted, but when he reached the third he could see that there was a large recess behind the cascading water. He found a path that allowed him to access the cavern without getting too wet. He had only taken a couple steps in when he came upon the very unlikely sight of a mermaid sitting against the limestone with a laptop propped up on her tail. Jack stared at her and time seemed to slow down. His memories hadn't done her justice. She was even more beautiful than he had remembered.

He exhaled and she looked up in alarm, letting out a small cry and moving towards the pool of water.

"Wait!" Jack called out, taking a step forward. The mermaid paused and her grey eyes roved over him. Jack suddenly felt very self conscious. He'd had plenty of girls tell him he was good looking before, but this was the first time it mattered.

"Oh, it's you," she finally said, cocking her head to the side.

Jack grinned, oddly thrilled that she remembered him. She looked as if she were about to smile back, but then her expression hardened.

"What are you doing here?"

Jack gulped. "I... I was patrolling the area, and I saw you, so I decided to come see if you were okay."

The mermaid narrowed her eyes at him. "Did Slightly send you? If he did, you can tell him I'd rather get swallowed by the cheetah whale than be in that ridiculous mermaid show."

Jack chuckled. "No, Slightly didn't send me. I actually wanted to talk to you."

She eyed him suspiciously but didn't say anything, so he continued.

"I just wanted to thank you for saving our lives from the other mermaids."

She made a face. "I didn't do it because I *cared* about any of you. It was just the right thing to do."

Jack shrugged. "Sure, but it must have been hard to go against your own kind."

She stiffened. "What do you mean my own kind?"

Jack winced, realizing he'd struck a nerve. "I just meant that you all spend so much time together, it must be like a sisterhood," he offered, hoping to appease her.

She relaxed a bit, but still looked perturbed. "I haven't been close to those girls in years," she said, a trace of sadness in her voice. "I haven't been close to *anybody* in years."

Jack was on the verge of telling her she could get as close to him as she wanted, but he thought it was a little early for cheesy statements like that. Instead he opted for something safer.

"I'm Jack, by the way."

She hesitated a moment before she responded. "I'm Cora."

For two glorious seconds she smiled at him, but then she looked like she was going to leave, so he searched his brain for something else to say.

"Hey, I also wanted to apologize if I overstepped my boundaries when I cut those ropes off of you.

Now it was Cora's turn to look self conscious. "Oh, that," she said, twisting her long black hair around her fingers. "I've developed a habit of being defensive."

"It's not a terrible habit to have," Jack said, venturing a step closer. "Although, I was unconscious for a couple days."

Cora bit her lip. "Really?"

"Yep. And when I woke up in the hospital I kept babbling on about Neverland, so they sent me to a mental institution for a week."

Her eyes went wide. "Seriously?"

"Yeah, it was pretty crazy."

She laughed at his joke, and it was a wonderful sound, even though it seemed a bit strained, like she hadn't laughed in a long time.

"Anyway," he continued, "it turned out to be a really interesting experience, so I guess I forgive you."

Cora's smile vanished. "You *forgive* me?" She exclaimed, slapping her purple tail against the water.

"Whoa, calm down!" Jack said, taking a step back. "I was just trying to be friendly!"

Apparently that was the wrong thing to say. Cora's face turned bright red with anger.

"Listen, Jack," she said, saying his name like it was a curse, "I don't need your forgiveness, I don't need your apologies, and I definitely don't need your friendship. You don't know me, and you never will, so please leave me alone!"

"Cora, wait!"

But the irate mermaid had already shut her laptop and slid into the water. He watched her dark purple tail disappear as she swam out into the lagoon.

"That went a lot differently than I had planned," Jack muttered to himself, finding his way out of the cavern. He reviewed their conversation, noting that it hadn't been all bad. He sighed. He should just give up. He should go find some nice girl in London to chase after. But no one had ever intrigued him like this. He had to find out more about her. It was just going to be a lot more difficult to approach her a second time. After all, she had made it very clear she didn't want to see him again. Her hostility and coldness should have repulsed him. Unfortunately, it only made him like her more.

Chapter Three

Lily quickly finished mopping the floor and gathered her things to leave the hospital. She was especially motivated to leave work early today because Slightly was making her dinner in Neverland. She smiled as she thought about the underground world that was becoming like a second home to her. She loved being there when the park was open, but being there after hours was an entirely different experience. With the crowds gone and only the people that lived there remaining, it somehow felt more magical, more captivating. On top of all that, she loved spending time with Slightly. He had been busy the last few weeks, but the few times they had been together had been filled with laughter and lively conversation. She felt peaceful when she was with him, which was a rare emotion in her life.

Lily changed out of her uniform, grabbed her bag, rushed out the front doors and nearly ran into her brother, Jason. She was about to scold him for bothering her at work, but then she saw the look on his face.

"Lily, I need to talk to you," he said in a hushed voice, his eyes full of fear.

Lily stared at her older brother. His anxiety was uncharacteristic. It took a lot to get him rattled, and Lily tried not to let dread overtake her as she took his arm and walked a few paces away from the hospital entrance.

"Make it quick, I have somewhere to be," she said, trying to sound casual. They walked a couple blocks in silence until Jason guided her into a dark alley.

"Jason, what's going on?"

His eyes darted all around before he pulled her farther down the alley. "Lily, the gang is very angry with you."

Lily exhaled in relief. "I knew that, Jason. You didn't have to come be all intense about it."

"No, Lily, it's worse than you think," he said, his fingers twitching in anxiety. "Why did you have to fight them?"

Lily groaned, recalling how she had taken on five boys at once, seriously injuring two of them. "They provoked me!" She exclaimed. "What was I supposed to do? Just let them beat me up?"

"No, you should have agreed to come back."

"I'm done with the gang. You know that."

Jason turned and kicked a wall. "You can't just leave the gang, Lily! They might have let you go with some bargaining, but then you attacked them, and now they're not going to stop until they find you."

"Okay, fine. I'll figure out a way to pay them off or something."

"It's too late for that. After what you did, they're not going to show any mercy." He looked into her eyes, his expression a mix of anger and grief. "Lily, they're going to kill you."

Chapter Four

Peter saw Wendy coming out of the lift that descended into Neverland and he ran to her. She beamed when she saw him coming and his heart soared. He lifted her up and spun her around, kissing her for a long moment before setting her back down on the ground again.

"Ew!"

A chorus of gagging sounds erupted behind them, and Peter turned to see a group of boys looking at them in disgust.

"Miss Wendy, did he spit in your mouth?"

"No, he kissed her," another boy piped up. "It's something people do when they grow up."

"Gross! I'm never going to grow up!"

"Alright boys, that's enough," Wendy said, her expression equal parts embarrassment and exhilaration.

"Where's Trevor?" Another one of the boys asked.

"He's doing battle games with Nibs in the jungle," Peter responded.

"Ooh! Can we go, Miss Wendy? Can we go?"

"Yes, but stay together," Wendy said. "Matthew and Arthur, you're in charge of keeping an eye on Zachary and Duke."

"Yes, Miss Wendy."

The boys took off towards the jungle, leaving Peter with Wendy. He bent down and kissed her again, and she kissed him back in a way that made it feel like they weren't surrounded by crowds of people. They broke apart and she winked at him, then took his hand and began walking down the path. It took several seconds for Peter to clear his head enough to notice where they were going.

Peter couldn't help but smile. The last two weeks had been euphoric. It had been a little stressful extracting the rest of Hook's treasure from the chambers in the lagoon and trying to manage the bakery and help run Neverland at the same time, but having Wendy back in his life had made Peter feel like anything was possible. She would usually come to Neverland twice a week with the boys from Mrs. Nancy's, and then she would often come back in the evenings after Neverland had closed.

"How's your mother?" Peter asked as they walked by Smee giving an exotic cooking demonstration.

Wendy shrugged. "She's fine. Her new job is at a hospital that's farther than she likes, but she's adjusting alright. To be honest, I think she misses working at the bakery. She's always talking about how fun it was."

Peter laughed. He wouldn't exactly call working with Wendy's mom *fun*, but she had been very helpful and he had enjoyed getting to know her a bit better. He had hired someone else to manage the bakery with Susan, and he only dropped in occasionally to make sure things were running smoothly.

He heard kids squealing with delight as they passed the animal arena where people were feeding the kangarabbits and lining up to take a ride on the Buffalostrich Rex. Finally they arrived at the section of the jungle where Nibs simulated battle games. Peter could see that Nibs was gearing up the boys to play Dead Man's Plaugue, and a few of them were being pretty careless with the pigment shooters.

Wendy frowned. "How long do the effects of those darts last again?"

"A couple hours," Peter responded. "Why?"

"I'd rather not return a bunch of multicolored boys to Mrs. Nancy."

Suddenly a small red-haired boy ran out from behind a zebra tree and rushed over to Wendy.

"Trevor!" She cried, kneeling down to embrace the boy. "How are you?"

"Great! I just created a walkway in the Imagination Tower! It massages your feet when you step on it, and Curly said they might keep it in the park! And last night I helped Slightly find some people that were hiding out in a cave!"

Peter shook his head. "Wait, what? Who was hiding out?"

Trevor's eyes glistened with excitement. "It was a boy and a girl. They were trying to spend the night, but Slightly told them they had to leave. Then they tried to fight, but Slightly's girlfriend took care of them."

"Slightly's girlfriend?"

"Yeah, Lily. She was amazing! She was running up walls and doing flips and she tied them up with her sweatshirt!"

Peter and Wendy looked at each other in alarm.

"I'd better go talk to Slightly," Peter said, giving Wendy's hand a squeeze. "I'll be back."

Peter found Slightly by the lagoon, reading a newspaper.

"Hey, I heard you had an exciting night yesterday."

Slightly blew out a breath. "Yeah. Somehow a couple visitors circumvented our closing security check. They resisted, but luckily Lily was there to help."

"Lily?"

Slightly blushed. "You've seen her around. She's that stunning girl with the long brown hair."

Peter smiled. He was glad that Slightly's foray into the Grey World had brought him so many good things.

"Anyway," Slightly went on, "we were having dinner on the beach when Trevor showed up and said he kept hearing noises near the caves. You probably know the rest."

Peter ran a hand through his hair. "Maybe we should hire a night guard."

Slightly furrowed his brows, but then a sly smile formed on his lips. "Jack would do it."

"Jack Baker? The guy with the great beard?"

Slightly nodded thoughtfully. "He does have a great beard, doesn't he? I have a feeling he'd have no problem changing shifts."

Peter shrugged. "If you think so, then that's settled."

Slightly nodded and gazed out at the water. "That's one problem solved."

"Is there another one?"

Slightly sighed. "Yeah." He held out the newspaper. "Have you seen this?"

Peter took the newspaper from Slightly and read the headline.

"Neverland mermaids stun audiences with incredible feats of showmanship."

"Well, that's good, isn't it?" Peter asked. "People are impressed with the mermaids."

Slightly looked down at the newspaper. "This reporter speculates the mermaids use wires or jet-powered tails to help them perform their stunts."

Peter snorted. "That's ridiculous. They're just using their natural skills."

"Except that those skills aren't natural."

"What do you mean?"

Slightly looked pained. "Mermaids don't exist. They're fictional, fantastical creatures."

Peter was about to laugh, but then he realized that in all the time he'd spent in the Grey World, he'd never heard anything about mermaids. He thought about how Wendy had reacted to them and about conversations he'd had with Cora that suddenly made a lot more sense. He felt nauseous as he grasped his ignorance.

Slightly nodded, reading the expression on Peter's face. "I felt pretty daft when I found out too."

Peter swallowed, trying to rid the dryness from his mouth. "Then how...?" He trailed off, squinting at the lagoon.

"I don't know," Slightly admitted, looking sober as he folded up the newspaper.

Peter stared at Slightly, then back out at the water. "That is a problem."

Chapter Five

Cora twisted the small pipe attached to her sleeping pod, but it still didn't work. She frowned and rested her head against the glass encasing her pod, wishing she had paid more attention the last time Nibs had fixed her pipe. Since all the mermaids needed air every two hours, they had special tubes leading into their sleeping enclosures that piped in bubbles. This way they didn't have to wake up constantly to go get air from the surface or the common room.

Cora rubbed her temples. It was late and she was exhausted, but if she didn't get her pipe fixed she would be having a very long night. She swam up to the surface, hoping someone would still be awake. Sometimes she would find Smee on the beach roasting rum berries over the fire.

She emerged several meters away from shore. The fabricated Neverland moon and stars glistened on the water, and for a moment, Cora felt something close to serenity. She noticed someone walking along the beach with a flashlight. It looked like Peter. She swam over to where he was and slid up on a rock.

"Hey! I need your help!"

He jumped and turned around. "Cora?"

She frowned. It wasn't Peter, it was that meddlesome security guard, Jack. The one she had hoped never to see again.

"I thought you were Peter," she grumbled.

He took a half step towards her. Cora couldn't read his expression, his hazel eyes were hidden in the darkness. She silently cursed herself for remembering the color of his eyes.

"Why are you here?" She demanded.

"I'm working," Jack replied. "They decided they wanted a night guard and they asked me." He ventured a step closer. "Why are you here?"

Cora sighed in frustration. "The air tube in my sleeping pod isn't working." She explained quickly. "I need Nibs or Peter to fix it. Could you please go get one of them?"

Jack inclined his head, and Cora could see the moonlight shining across his strong features.

"I thought you could breathe underwater."

Cora resisted the urge to growl. She was a bit defensive that he was bringing up her abnormalities. "I can. I just have to get air every two hours."

Jack nodded. "That makes sense."

Cora tensed. This boy continued to infuriate her. Nothing about her situation made sense, and here he was, acting as if he understood her composition. It made her sick.

"Would you please go get Nibs or Peter?" She repeated through gritted teeth.

"Of course," he responded genially. He turned and walked away.

Cora almost fell asleep on the rock while she waited. The only thing that kept her awake was her frustration that she'd be seeing more of Jack if he was going to be the night guard. After about 20 minutes she heard a noise and was enraged to see Jack returning with some tools and a forever breathe mask.

"Peter's in London tonight and Nibs didn't want to get out of bed, so he gave me the instructions and told me to do it."

Cora was instantly filled with feelings of fear and indignation. She didn't want some stranger seeing where she lived.

"No," she said adamantly, slapping her tail against the rock.

Jack looked unsure of himself. He opened his mouth, but before he could say anything, Cora cut in.

"It's a private place down there. I'd like to get this problem fixed, but just because some ruggedly handsome jerk offers his help doesn't mean that I'm going to let him into my bed!"

Jack quirked an eyebrow in amusement and Cora groaned. It had come out all wrong.

"That's not what I meant," she grumbled. "I just don't like strangers in my space."

"Not even ruggedly handsome ones?"

Cora rolled her eyes. Why did he have to pick out the compliment from the insult?

"Just tell me how," she demanded. "I'll do it myself."

Jack shook his head. "It's a two person job. I have to go with you. Unless you'd like to ask one of the other mermaids."

As much as she hated taking Jack to the bottom of the lagoon, Cora knew none of the other mermaids would help her. For a moment she considered sleeping in the common room, but the last time she did that she had a back ache for a week.

"Fine," she said, sliding down into the water.

Jack secured the tools on his belt and stepped into the water.

"Are you going to wear that?" She asked, eying him skeptically.

He laughed, and the pleasant sound of it took Cora by surprise. "Would you like me to take off my clothes?"

Cora suppressed a scream of frustration. This guy was really getting under her skin, and it was rare that she ever got this unsettled. "Let's just get this over with," she muttered and dove into the water.

She swam slowly so he could keep up, but then she realized she didn't have to. She was impressed that he was such a strong swimmer. He only had to pause once to equalize his ears as they went deeper into the lagoon. Once or twice he shined his flashlight on a big fish or in the spires of the mermaids' home, but mostly he kept next to her and shined the light straight ahead. When they arrived at her sleeping pod, he anchored himself to it by wrapping his leg around one of the posts.

He motioned for her to hold the glass encasing of the pod open with one hand while steadying the air pipe with the other. She watched him pry off the motor and then use a tiny screwdriver to replace and tighten the fasteners. She was amazed that his big fingers were nimble enough to handle such small tools. Finally, he replaced the motor and she helped him guide the pipe through it. A few seconds later, the pipe was generating small air bubbles again.

Cora quickly swam into the sleeping pod and shut the case, eager to put something between them. She signed thank you and then waved a very deliberate goodbye. It was hard to see his face behind the forever breathe mask, but she thought she detected a small smile. He checked the motor one more time, then nodded and swam away. Cora turned in her pod and tried to go to sleep, but she was so riled up that she knew it would be a while before she could finally drift off.

Chapter Six

Jack was elated. He knew the mermaids lived in the lagoon, but he never imagined that their home would be so incredible. After he had left Cora, he went to explore some of the other rooms and areas of their exquisite underwater compound. He kept his light low so that he wouldn't disturb the other mermaids in their sleeping pods. He swam from place to place, discovering elaborate mechanical systems and areas that appeared to be dedicated to playing games and making crafts. But the most awe-inspiring features were the walls made out of beautiful jewels and stones, and the glass spires that surrounded the structures.

After a few more minutes of looking around, he started to swim back up to the surface. He felt quite at home in the water. It reminded him of his days of competitive swimming. He passed some exotic fish and then came upon something huge. He carefully shined his light on what appeared to be a whale with cheetah skin. Mesmerized, he swam around to the other side to inspect the creature. It seemed to be furry, so he reached out to touch it. Suddenly, the whale quivered and its gigantic tail swung around and slapped Jack away. The impact of the tail was so great that it knocked off his forever breathe mask and he lost hold of his flashlight. He quickly swam away in case the whale struck again, but there was no sign of his mask, and his flashlight was quickly falling to the bottom of the lagoon. Now with limited air, he attempted to swim towards the surface, but he was disoriented and couldn't tell which way was up. He floundered for several moments until finally he caught a glimpse of the moon. He swam towards it, but he was getting light headed and it seemed so far away. His legs were burning and every stroke was a struggle, and then his faculties failed him. He floated in the dark water and experienced a second of peaceful bliss before he passed out.

*****

Jack came to with a violent cough. His head felt like it was going to explode and his right shoulder was throbbing with pain.

"Oh good, you're alive. I was considering giving you mouth to mouth resuscitation, but the thought of it was so repulsive that I might have just let you die."

Jack sat up and coughed a few more times, then focused on Cora, who was sitting next to him on the beach and giving him a hateful glare. "I should have stayed out longer, then," he said weakly. "I would have taken my chances."

Cora flipped her tail around and hit him in his injured shoulder. He fell back and grunted in pain.

"Enough!" He cried, propping himself back up. "I've had enough of being battered by tails for one night!"

"Didn't anyone ever tell you not to touch a whale?" Cora said mockingly. "What were you thinking?"

"I wasn't," Jack admitted. "That was stupid. I was just so intrigued by it."

"Well, from now on, you should suppress your curiosity," Cora muttered. "I'm sure it's all very *fascinating*, but maybe you should mind your own business."

Jack peered into her unyielding grey eyes. He knew she wasn't talking about the whale anymore.

"How did you know I was in trouble?" He asked softly.

She clenched her jaw and hesitated a few seconds before she answered. "I could feel it."

"*Feel* it?"

She tossed her hair over her shoulder in irritation. "Yes, I felt it. When something as large as the cheetah whale moves in the water, it's hard not to notice the vibrations."

Jack took a deep breath. He had a million questions, but he decided to keep them to himself.

"Well, thank you for saving me. Again."

Cora's tail flinched. "I didn't do it for you."

"I know, I know," Jack said, waving his hand in the air. "It was the right thing to do. I'm just glad you have a hero complex."

Cora turned and stared at him. Even in the darkness, Jack could see the anger on her face. Unfortunately, the livid expression did nothing to diminish her appeal.

"You are so... I just can't... Ugh!" She ended her incoherent rant by pulling herself angrily towards the water and swimming away. Jack sighed. The more he learned about

Cora, the more he was drawn to her, but it seemed the attraction was definitely not mutual.

*****

"Looks like we have some trouble down at the mermaid show," Tink informed Jack through his earpiece.

"I'll be there in a minute."

Jack rubbed his eyes as he walked down the stairs of the Imagination Tower. He was exhausted. He had gone home that morning and slept only a few hours before Slightly had called him in to fill in for another guard who was sick. Not only was he tired, but he was also still sore from his adventures in the lagoon the night before.

He smiled as he remembered his interactions with Cora, even though most of the time she had been hostile towards him. He didn't know why everything he did angered her, although he supposed he could have reigned in some of his comments. He had a genuine interest in her, and not because she had a tail and lived in the water. He just wanted to get to know her. Was that really so offensive? At least she had called him handsome and saved his life, so there had to be some positive feelings there, even if they were minuscule.

When he got to the beach he saw that the show had ended, but the mermaids weren't visiting with the fans like usual. Instead, they were grouped together a few meters away from the shore while Slightly struggled with a large man who looked like he was trying to jump into the water. Jack rushed over and grabbed the man's wrist, twisting it until he buckled over in pain. Jack didn't have any handcuffs, but he did have some zip ties, which he used to tie the man's hands behind his back.

"What happened?" Jack asked Slightly, keeping a firm grip on the man's arm.

"The mermaids were taking pictures with the visitors, and he tried to pull one of them out of the water."

"It was Nerissa!" The man interjected. "She's the love of my life! We're meant to be together!"

"I don't think so, sir," Slightly said with a worried expression.

"But I love her! You don't understand!"

"Oh, but I do," Jack muttered, tightening his grip on the man's arm.

"I don't care that she lives in the water! We'll make it work!"

Slightly shifted uncomfortably. "Of course she doesn't live in the water."

"Please," the man spat. "All you have to do is look at those mermaids to know they're real."

Jack and Slightly shared a look of alarm.

"I'll let our costumer know she's doing an excellent job," Slightly lied.

They listened to him babble on for a few minutes more until the police came to escort him out of the park. Slightly followed the police to file a report, leaving Jack alone next to the water.

"Thanks for getting rid of that scary guy."

Jack jumped. He hadn't noticed the small mermaid with the gold tail approaching.

"Sure," Jack responded. "Your safety is very important."

The mermaid giggled. "I'm Isla, by the way."

"Nice to meet you."

She smiled and batted her eyelashes, and Jack realized she was flirting with him. If only he could get Cora to do that. When she kept smiling at him, he figured he'd try to find out some answers.

"So, do you enjoy performing for everyone?" He asked.

"Oh, yes! I love it! It makes things so much more exciting than before!"

Jack glanced around to make sure no one was listening. "Can I ask you where you're from?"

Isla giggled again. "The lagoon, of course."

Jack leaned down closer to her. "Right, but have you always lived there?"

"No."

"So, where were you before you came to Neverland?"

Isla frowned. "It was so long ago, the details are hazy. I remember being in an orphanage when I was really young, and then Mrs. Carnivera came and took me to a hospital or something. Then I think I was asleep for a really long time and when I woke up I was a mermaid."

Jack raised his eyebrows. "So, you weren't a mermaid before you came here?"

"No, silly! None of us were!" She said with a laugh.

Right then another mermaid with a bright green tail swam up next to Isla. "Hey Isla, Nerissa wants you to console her. She's pretty shaken up about that man."

"Oh, okay." Isla waved goodbye to Jack and swam off with the other mermaid.

Jack rubbed his forehead as he considered what Isla had just told him. Something about the whole situation was off. All of these girls had been taken and altered, and he doubted it was because some crazy person just wanted to have magical creatures swimming around in a lagoon. There had to be some greater purpose to the creation of these mermaids, and he sensed that it was a dangerous one.

Chapter Seven

Cora was doing some work on her laptop in the common room when the other mermaids came swimming up through the entrance. They appeared shaken up about something and were all talking at once. Except for a glance or two in her direction, they didn't acknowledge that Cora was even there.

"I can't believe that man attacked you!" Piper exclaimed, putting her hand on Nerissa's shoulder. "Are you okay?"

"I think I'll be alright," Nerissa responded, wiping away tears that weren't there. "I think I just have to re-evaluate who I engage with."

Cora rolled her eyes. *This ought to be good*, she thought.

"I remember that man from a few days ago," Nerissa continued. "His name was John Olsen. He had seemed nice, but he wouldn't stop asking me questions, and he wasn't very good looking. I shouldn't have talked to him in the first place."

Catalina nodded vigorously. "From now on, we should only talk to cute guys under the age of 21."

"Maybe 22 if they're really attractive," Piper interjected.

"Yeah, guys like Mason Harper," Meredith said dreamily, and Nerissa gave her a fierce look.

"Mason Harper is mine, Meredith," Nerissa said sharply. "I claimed him yesterday."

"I know," Meredith said, "but I can still admire him, can't I?"

Nerissa narrowed her eyes, but then shrugged. "I suppose."

Isla frowned. "Who is Mason Harper?"

"Only the best looking guy in all existence," Meredith replied, drumming her fingers on her heart. "Dark hair, crystal blue eyes, and a smile to die for."

"And he's really nice," Piper added.

"And he's *mine*," Nerissa said with a flick of her pink tail that effectively silenced the other mermaids for a few seconds.

"Well, I don't know about you guys," Isla finally said with a shy smile, "but I think Jack Baker is really attractive."

Cora flinched at the mention of the boy she hated.

"The security guard?" Catalina asked. "With the red hair?"

"There's nothing wrong with red hair," Piper said defensively.

"Yeah," Isla responded. "He's just so manly. I feel like he could protect me from anything. And I think he's interested in me."

An odd twinge of pain rippled through Cora, but she quickly suppressed the feeling and passed it off as surprise.

"I don't know," Piper said, chewing on her fingernail, "he's kind of hairy. That beard..."

"Oh, his beard is perfect!" Isla said with a giggle. "Not too long, not too short."

Meredith nodded. "I could bury my fingers in a good beard."

The rest of them gave her a strange look and Nerissa cleared her throat. "Well, Isla, you have my permission to like him if you want, but he seems a bit weird to me."

"Absolutely, I agree," Cora said suddenly. "That guy is completely unstable."

Nerissa gasped and gave Cora a murderous look. "Nobody asked you, Cora!" She yelled, then turned and swam out of the common room. The other mermaids dutifully followed her.

Cora shrugged and went back to working on her laptop. She was getting tired of their asinine conversation anyway.

*****

Cora swam as fast as she could towards the inlet where the jungle and the cliffs bordered the lagoon. Trying to decipher what Lina, her dolphin friend, was trying to tell her had been a bit difficult, but she had gotten the essence of the message. Blue, the other dolphin, was in mortal danger.

Cora had learned to communicate with the two dolphins in the lagoon early during her time in Neverland.

Since the other mermaids had been ostracizing her for years, she worked on befriending the dolphins and had developed a good sense of their language. Often, she found that the conversations she had with the dolphins were far more interesting and intellectual than those she had with the other mermaids.

She reached the inlet and found that Blue was tangled up in the plastic netting they used to keep visitors out of the lagoon. The barrier was generally effective until the Buffalostrich Rex came along and ate through it, spitting the residue into the water. Cora swam up to the struggling dolphin and tried to calm him. Lina hung behind, swimming back and forth in an anxious manner. Once Blue was relatively still, Cora worked her fingers through the netting, breaking it when necessary to free the dolphin's flippers and dorsal fin.

Finally, when Cora had removed all of the netting, Blue swam free and brushed up against her in gratitude. She followed the dolphins up to the surface where they bobbed their heads at her, whistling and clicking their thanks. She whistled a message back that loosely meant, "It was nothing." Cora watched the two dolphins swim away and was about to follow them when a heavy rod hit her on the shoulder. She spun around in anger and found a young man standing at the edge of the cliffs with a look of surprise on his face.

"What do you think you're..." her words and her fury faded as she took in the young man standing before her. Jet black hair, crystal blue eyes, and a smile to die for. She couldn't remember ever seeing anyone with such white teeth.

"Were you... talking to those dolphins?" He asked her, his eyes wide open in amazement.

"Maybe," Cora responded. She knew she should swim away, but she was captivated by his strong, cleft chin.

"That's incredible. You must have a lot of free time on your hands."

"You have no idea," Cora said before she could stop the words from coming out of her mouth.

He smiled at her and she thought that her insides might melt.

"You must be Mason," Cora blurted, wanting to slap herself for being so awkward.

He raised his eyebrows. "Indeed, I am. How did you know? Can you read minds as well as talk to dolphins?"

Cora laughed, but it came out stilted. "No. It's just that the other girls are quite enamored with you."

Mason chuckled and looked at the ground. "I see. But the real question is whether *you* are enamored with me. It seems your estimation is the only one that matters."

Cora's jaw dropped, but she quickly closed it. She felt as if her heart was doing flips in her chest.

"It's really too early to draw any conclusions," she said, hoping that her unsteady voice didn't betray the fact that she was most definitely enamored with him.

"I've got my work cut out for me, then," Mason replied with a wink. "And I regret to say that I'll have to start it by asking you a favor, but first, I have a question."

"Of course, ask me anything." *Ugh, could I sound any more desperate?* She thought.

"I couldn't help but notice that you're not in the show with the other mermaids. Why is that?"

Cora hesitated. A part of her wanted to share all of her secrets with this gorgeous stranger, but she hadn't quite lost her sense of self preservation. "I'm shy. Being in front of a crowd is difficult for me, and I'm not really comfortable showing myself to the world."

"That's a pity," Mason replied, looking at her so intensely it seemed he was boring holes through to her soul. "So, you're afraid."

"You could say that, yes."

He studied her a moment longer. "But it's not because you're shy."

"What makes you say that?"

"You're afraid that everyone will find out what you really are. That you're not just some beautiful girl who dons a tail for a few hours a day, but that this is, in fact, your life and your world. You proved this by not participating in the show, for why would they hire a girl to pretend to be a mermaid if she's not going to entertain and engage with the guests?"

"Th-That's an interesting theory," she stammered, "but they're still working on my role. I'll be doing more intimate interactions."

"Even if that were the case, it still wouldn't explain how the other mermaids are able to jump so high or hold their breath for so long. And in my brief conversations with them, even though they don't divulge much, I've deduced that they do, in fact, live at the bottom of this lagoon."

Cora began to shake. Here it was. Everything she feared had been found out in just a few observations.

Mason must have seen the shock on her face because he held up his hands in a gesture of peace. "Don't worry, I'm not going to tell anyone. I'm actually more interested in protecting all of you. Believe me, I know how it feels to be looked at as different and unnatural." He lifted up his pant leg to reveal a large, metal boot in place of his calf and foot. "I was in the military for a short time," he explained, "it happened in an unfortunate conflict."

He gazed mournfully at his metal foot, and Cora's heart went out to him. The others hadn't mentioned that he was missing half a limb. Mason apparently thought this feature made him less attractive, but it only made Cora like him more.

"Which brings me to that favor," he said, shaking off his morose mood with a small smile. "I wandered over here because I was following an exquisite mechanical wolf. Then I saw you and those dolphins, and I was so surprised that I dropped my crutch which, regrettably, hit your shoulder before it sank to the bottom of the lagoon. Would it be too much to ask you to retrieve it for me?"

"Oh, so you're just using me for my tail," Cora joked, hoping it wasn't too much.

"Yes, at this moment, I am."

Cora smiled and dove into the water, easily locating the crutch and bringing it back up to the surface.

"You are magnificent," Mason said, bending down and taking the crutch from Cora. His eyes locked on hers. "Thank you so much. You can't imagine how much I rely on this silly stick."

"We all have our weaknesses," Cora said breathlessly.

Mason gave her a charming half smile. "And I fear you are bringing out too many of mine."

He held her gaze for a few seconds more, and then stepped back and situated his crutch underneath his arm. "It has been enchanting to meet you... oh dear, I don't even know your name and yet I feel as though I've known you my entire life."

"It's Cora."

"What a lovely name."

"Thank you."

"Well, Cora, I'd better get back to my group, but would it be too forward to ask if I could see you again?"

Cora nearly jumped out of the water. "Not at all. I have a pretty open schedule."

Mason chuckled. "I suppose you do. I have to work all day tomorrow, but how about the next day, Friday? Perhaps we can meet here again, around 4:00?"

"Sounds perfect."

Mason winked at her again then turned and disappeared into the jungle. Cora felt like she should slap herself for being so idiotically lovestruck, but she couldn't help that the thought of Mason Harper made her smile more than she had in years.

Chapter Eight

"I don't know if it's an animal or a person, but we keep seeing evidence of suspicious activity from the north end of the forest at night," Tink said, showing Slightly the video footage of the area. "I can catch movements here and there, but I can't figure out what's causing it."

Slightly studied the video, watching leaves and bushes seeming to move of their own accord. It was almost as if a ghost were in the forest.

"I'll have Jack patrol the area," Slightly said, sitting back. "But it might just be a stray squirrel or something."

Tink chewed on her lip. "It seems to be more than that, but we'll see."

Slightly sat back in his chair and glanced at all the feeds coming into central control. "How are you doing?" He asked. "Do you like being the eyes and ears of Neverland?"

Tink gave him a sheepish grin. "I love it, actually. It's fascinating to watch all the people, and I love being in control."

Slightly laughed. "Well, you've always been good at bossing people around."

Tink threw one of her desk plants at him, but she was smiling. Slightly was glad that with everything else he had on his plate, he didn't have to deal with Tink being angry about opening Neverland up to the public. To say he was overwhelmed at the moment was an understatement. It seemed they were getting more and more visitors every day, which was great, but it meant that they were constantly short on personnel, and it really elevated Slightly's stress level. Plus, in two days they were hosting a big donor luncheon for everyone who had helped open the park. On top of that, he'd had multiple media requests to interview the mermaids, and he was running out of excuses.

"Hey, what do you know about the mermaids?" He asked.

Tink made a face. "They're annoying."

"No, I mean, do you know anything about how they got here, how they got... tails?"

Tink leaned back in her chair. "Oh. Well, I assume the Crocodile brought them. Other than that, I really don't know. Although, I did find this file-"

She was cut off by loud screaming coming from one of the feeds. Slightly stood and walked over to a screen showing the animal arena where a young girl was holding her hand and crying.

"You better go check that out," Tink said.

"Yep," Slightly answered, already heading out the door.

He ran to the arena and found a crowd gathered around the girl. Before he even entered the arena he could see that her hand was bleeding. The twins were trying to restrain an overactive kangarabbit and keep Lamar away from the crowd at the same time. After checking on the girl to make sure the wound wasn't too serious, he turned to the twins.

"What happened?" Slightly asked.

"This kangarabbit bit that girl's hand," one of the twins responded. "Her mother claims she didn't provoke it," the twin lowered his voice, "but I'm pretty sure she was feeding it some cheese puffs."

"Did you call Smee?"

"Yeah. He should be here any... oh, there he is."

Slightly saw Smee come loping through the arena, taking off his apron and putting on some sterile gloves.

"I was in the middle of a sushi demonstration," he said breathlessly. "Where is she?"

Slightly led Smee to the girl and watched the old pirate hastily put a bandage around her hand.

"You should probably use a disinfectant for an animal bite."

Slightly turned around and was surprised to see Lily right behind him. "Lily, where did you come from?"

"I just got off work, so I thought I'd come down."

"You're off work this early?"

"They changed my shift," she replied, not quite meeting Slightly's eyes.

He knew she was lying, but he didn't really have time to delve into it at the moment.

"Disinfectant, you say?"

"Yeah. Do you guys keep any antibiotic ointment on hand?"

Slightly winced. He knew they should have an assortment of first aid supplies, but he just hadn't had time for it.

Lily read his expression and nodded. "How about raw honey?"

"We've got that!" One of the twins piped up. "We just started beekeeping last week!" The twin ran to get the honey and came back a few minutes later with a cup of it. Lily took the honey over to the girl and soothed her as she undid the bandage and applied it to her wound, then expertly tied the bandage up again. The girl and her mother expressed their appreciation to her and left the arena.

"How did you know to do that with the honey?" Slightly asked Lily when she walked back over.

"My mother taught me," Lily replied. "There are a ton of plants and natural substances with healing properties."

Slightly stared at her, amazed by her knowledge. "Wow, do you want a job here?" He asked jokingly.

"Yes, I do," Lily replied quickly.

Slightly's eyebrows shot up in surprise. "Really? What about the hospital?"

Lily shrugged. "Oh, I'm pretty sick of that job. Plus, it'd be a lot better if I could be helping people instead of cleaning rooms."

Slightly nodded. Right now Smee was the stand in medic, and he was sure he wouldn't mind being relieved of those responsibilities so he could focus solely on his cooking demonstrations.

"Okay," Slightly said, "do you need a couple weeks to notify the hospital?"

"No, I can start tomorrow," Lily replied, practically stumbling over her words. "My position can be filled easily," she added.

"If that works for you, that'd be wonderful."

"Great! I'll work on getting some supplies together," she said with a wink that made Slightly's breath catch in his throat. She gave him a quick hug and then ran off towards the entrance.

Slightly couldn't help smiling. He was excited at the prospect of spending more time with Lily. Plus, with her being around more often, he thought he might be able to figure out what she was hiding.

Chapter Nine

Jack was having a hard time paying attention to what Tink was trying to tell him. He was sitting in a chair across from her in her small office in central control, and his eyes kept wandering to the many screens that were displaying what was happening in different parts of Neverland. In addition, a pair of creepy, animatronic birds were singing in the corner, and they were horribly distracting. He didn't know how Tink got anything done. He shook his head and forced himself to look at what Tink was showing him.

"Look at this section over here," Tink said, pointing to a video of the forest from the night before. "There was a little bit of a breeze, so the leaves are moving, but the leaves on this tree are moving the other way. And the other night, when I turned the volume up, I could hear breathing."

"Breathing?"

"Yes. Heavy, labored breathing."

Jack frowned. "Maybe It was a deer or something."

"Deer don't breathe like that. I think we have an intruder."

Jack sighed. "So you want me to check it out?"

"Yes, please."

"Alright." Jack stood up and looked at the screen again. "Where exactly is this? On the northern edge of the forest?"

"By the Weather Tree."

"Okay." He was about to leave when something from another one of the screens caught his eye. "Whoa, what is this?" He walked over and turned up the volume on a video showing Cora talking to some pretty boy by the cliffs.

"I wouldn't do that, Jack," Tink warned. "It'll only bring you pain."

But it was too late. With just a few keystrokes, he was listening to a conversation that, according to the time stamp, had happened yesterday afternoon. Jack quickly became disgusted with the guy and his smooth words, but what was more alarming was that Cora seemed to be smitten with him.

"Who is that?" He asked, turning to Tink.

"Mason Harper," Tink replied. "He's visited the park three or four times now, and all the mermaids are in love with him, including Cora, apparently." She tapped her fingernails on the desk. "I was surprised. I thought she was stronger than that."

"So did I," Jack muttered.

Tink gave him a pitying look. "I wouldn't lose hope just yet," she said. "Maybe he'll turn out to be an awful person, and then you can have another chance."

Jack swallowed hard. "Wait. You know that I... like her?"

Tink quirked an eyebrow and gestured to all of the screens. "What do you think?"

Jack groaned and Tink held up her hands in defense.

"Hey, I can't help that watching Cora yell at you is way more interesting than watching Noodler pick his nose. I liked what you said about the mouth to mouth resuscitation, by the way. That was very funny."

"Okay, stop," Jack said, rubbing his forehead. "Does anyone else know?"

"No, I haven't told anyone. Oh, except Curly. We actually watched that whole beach scene together a few times. It was very entertaining."

Jack glared at her and she made an obvious effort to stop smiling.

"I'm sorry. I won't tell anyone else. For what it's worth, I'm rooting for you."

"Gee, thanks," Jack said sarcastically.

Tink folded her arms. "Do you know what would be a great distraction for you right now?"

"What?"

"Hunting down an intruder in the forest."

*****

Jack tried to get the image of Cora gazing dreamily at that guy out of his mind, but it seemed to be burned into his memory. He grumbled about fickle mermaids as he walked through the forest, only half-heartedly looking for the supposed intruder. He was so consumed with his embittered thoughts that he almost didn't hear the gasp. He froze and peered into the darkness, wondering if he had just imagined the sound. He was reaching for his flashlight when he noticed some rustling in the hedge to his right. He took a cautious step towards it, and suddenly the hedge shook violently as something bolted out of it. Jack took off running, following the fleeing footsteps. He couldn't quite make out what he was pursuing because of the darkness and the heavily wooded forest, but he thought every now and then he caught a glimpse of some hair or an arm.

Finally, he emerged into a small clearing surrounded by large trees, but there was no sign of the intruder. Jack walked all around the perimeter of the clearing and behind all the trees, but the mysterious trespasser seemed to have vanished.

Chapter Ten

"But we like taking pictures with the guests," Alf Mason complained. "It gets us more tips."

"And it makes us feel like we're famous," Whibbler added with a gleeful grin.

Slightly held his head in his hands, wondering how these pirates could be so inane. Nearly all the pirates gave daily tours to visitors on the ship, and Slightly was sitting with them now, addressing the issue of their notoriety.

"You don't have the luxury of being famous," Slightly said, rubbing his eyes, "because you're all still wanted criminals." He stood up and paced the deck of the ship. "Tink has erased your records, but the more your pictures circulate through London, the more likely it will be that someone will recognize you."

"Hm, I never thought of that," Starkey said, scratching his ear.

"That's why you need to either decline pictures, or wear your disguises."

Alf Mason groaned. "But those beards are so itchy and uncomfortable!"

"They're more comfortable than jail," Bill Jukes said, giving a meaningful look to Alf Mason.

"Exactly," Slightly said.

"Alright, boy, you've made your point," Cecco grumbled. "Now leave us alone."

Slightly happily obliged, walking down the ship's ramp and wading through the water until he arrived on the beach.

He sighed and sat on a rock, looking out at the lagoon in the moonlight. Things were going pretty well in Neverland, and everything was in place for the donor luncheon the following day, but he couldn't shake the feeling that something awful was about to happen. There were just too many variables he couldn't control. Just then he heard someone walking up behind him. He turned around and saw Jack Baker approaching.

"Hey, I have a question for you," Jack said, sitting down next to Slightly on the rock.

"Sure, what's up?"

"Have the twins been experimenting with any new animals or hybrids? Possibly ones with the ability to become invisible?"

"Not that I know of. Why?"

"I just chased something through the forest that seemed to have disappeared. I don't know if it was a human or an animal, but it was incredibly quick and agile."

Slightly sat up a little straighter. Those adjectives seemed a little too familiar. "Really? Where exactly was this?"

"In the north part of the forest. Close to a clearing of large trees."

Slightly nodded, imagining the spot in his head. "I'll take a look over there," he said, standing up.

"Okay, but be careful. I've never seen anything like it."

Slightly trekked over to the forest, wondering if his theory would be correct. If it was, he wasn't sure if he sure be angry or excited. He reached the clearing that Jack had described and slowly walked around all the trees. He stopped to study one with a particularly large trunk and noticed a long crack near the base. He took a deep breath, bent down, pried open the base of the trunk, and found himself staring at a beautiful girl with long brown hair and almond shaped eyes.

"Hello Lily."

*****

"What were you thinking? I just can't imagine why you would do this!"

"Slightly, please let me explain."

After the initial shock had worn off and Slightly had urged Lily out of her hideaway, he had taken her to the Imagination Tower where they could talk privately, although he knew that Tink was probably watching.

"How long have you been staying in that tree?"

Lily sat down and stared out the expansive windows. "Four days."

"What?"

"Listen," Lily pleaded. The sincerity in her eyes made Slightly feel guilty for raising his voice. "I'm sorry. I know I should have talked to you in the first place, but I didn't want to burden you with my problems when you were already so overwhelmed."

Slightly shook his head. He knew he'd do anything for this girl, even though she was exhibiting some pretty crazy behavior. "I have been busy, but you have to know how much I care about you, Lily. I haven't exactly been hiding my feelings."

Lily allowed herself a small smile before the anxiety returned to her face. "I'm in trouble."

"What kind of trouble?"

Lily bit her lip. "The gang I used to be in, they're after me."

"What do you mean?"

"I guess I angered them when I fought back that day when you saw me, and now they want to kill me."

Slightly was speechless. He would have suggested that she report it to the police, but he knew that the situation was complicated and the law might not be the best option. He sat down and wrapped his arms around her.

"I don't want to endanger you or anyone here, but I don't know what else to do!" She cried.

He held her as she sobbed into his shirt, wishing that he could offer her a sensible solution. "We'll figure something out," he said softly. "In the meantime, you are welcome to stay in Neverland, but we need to find you some more suitable living quarters."

Lily sniffed and looked up at him. "I don't know, that tree trunk was actually quite cozy."

Chapter Eleven

"Why didn't you tell me there would be so many attractive young men here? I would have worn something more appealing."

Peter rolled his eyes as Susan passed by with a tray of sandwiches. The bakery was catering the luncheon, and Peter had recruited several people to help out, including all the lost boys and Wendy.

"Hey, are there any more of those cream puffs?" Wendy asked, brushing up against Peter's shoulder. "The mayor is asking for them."

Peter rushed into their staging tent and brought out a plate of cream puffs. He presented them to Wendy with a flourish.

"Here you are, Miss Darling," he said, winking at her.

Wendy raised her eyebrows in amusement. "No wonder my mother enjoyed working with you." She kissed his cheek before taking the plate and heading towards the mayor's table.

Peter watched her for a moment before turning back to the sheet cake he was cutting. The luncheon seemed to be going well, even though Slightly kept running around acting like the sky arch was about to collapse on them. He had told Peter that some of the most important people in London were there, but Peter wasn't too worried about it. He had learned while working in the bakery that if you treat everyone the same, it all works out just fine. Peter looked out at the beach where they had set up dozens of tables under a large, decorated canopy. Curly had engineered several water fountains that were planted in the sand and spurted out in various shapes. The twins were walking around with two trained monkeys that were performing tricks. Nibs had a high precision water gun that he was using to refill everyone's drinks from the shore. At first the guests were a bit shocked by beverages flying over their heads and into their glasses, but soon they were thrilled by it. At the moment, Nibs seemed to be studying Susan as she walked around the tables serving sandwiches.

Just then, Wendy came back with an empty tray.

"What can I do for you Miss Darling?" Peter asked playfully.

Wendy smiled mischievously. "Well, Mr..." she trailed off, the corners of her mouth turning downward.

"What's wrong?" Peter asked.

"I just realized I don't know your last name."

Peter laughed. "It's Mitchell."

Wendy made a face. "Mitchell? Really? I thought it'd be something like Smith, or Parker, or Pan."

Peter frowned. "Pan? Peter Pan? That sounds ridiculous."

Wendy shrugged. "I think it's catchy."

"Maybe. Sounds like a superhero or something."

Wendy quirked an eyebrow. "Well, Mr. Mitchell, I would like a kiss."

Peter's temperature warmed a few degrees. "Gladly," he said, leaning forward. But before he could kiss her, he noticed Nibs and Susan heading towards the staging tent at the same time. They weren't paying attention and they collided with one another. Nibs tried to keep hold of his beverage gun and ended up squirting liquid all over Susan's shirt.

"Watch where you're going, you little troll!" Susan yelled.

Nibs dusted himself off and looked Susan in the eye, even though he was a head shorter than her. "Trolls are often depicted as strong and strategic," so I'll take that as a compliment.

"You wish!" Susan scoffed. "And don't think I haven't noticed you staring at me! Are you in love with me or something?"

Nibs crossed his arms over his chest. "You are very beautiful, but I could not possibly love you after merely an hour. Love is an emotion that must be crafted and refined day after day, and my love could never go to someone so unworthy of it. You have a strong appearance but a weak mind. You seem only to think of yourself and refuse to develop your potential. There is no possible way I could love you as you are right now, but maybe in time."

Susan's jaw dropped and her eyes filled with fire. "Don't you ever speak to me again, you hideous twit!"

She stomped off and Nibs shrugged. He turned to face Peter and Wendy, who had watched the entire exchange.

"So, I see you've met Susan," Peter said hesitantly.

Nibs gave a small nod. His expression was as stoic as ever, except for a slight gleam in his eye. "She's got spirit. I like her."

Chapter Twelve

Cora sat in front of a mirror in the common room, attempting to style her hair. She had tried a dozen ways, but none of them seemed quite right. She was going up to the inlet to meet Mason in a few minutes and she wanted to look perfect.

For the past two days her thoughts had been filled with Mason, even though she realized that in their interaction she hadn't learned much about him. She had spent a lot of time in the common room, hoping she would overhear the other mermaids talking about him. They had mentioned him a few times, but it was only to comment on his dreamy eyes and gorgeous smile. Oddly, none of them brought up his missing foot.

Cora sighed and shook her hair out of the braid she had started. She'd just leave her hair down, it was more comfortable that way. She glanced at her reflection one more time, then swam down the room's tunnel and out of the gate.

*****

"I didn't know what you liked to eat, so I brought a variety."

Cora laughed as she looked at the spread of food and snacks that Mason had set out on a small blanket. There was shrimp, sushi, nuts, scones, small sandwiches, and crab salad.

"Thank you," Cora said, taking a handful of almonds, "but I should tell you now that I don't eat fish."

Mason slapped his palm to his forehead. "Of course you don't! How insensitive of me!"

"It's fine! Don't worry about it."

"Well, I hope you don't mind if I eat fish, because this sushi is divine."

Mason winked and Cora felt her cheeks warm. He was sitting on the ground with his legs stretched out, his metal boot prominently catching the light. He had carefully propped his crutch against a rock away from the water. At Mason's suggestion, Cora had come out of the water and was sitting next to him with her tail in full view. At first this had made her nervous, but Mason had a way of putting her at ease.

"So Cora," Mason said, putting his hand on her tail in a way that was terrifying and exciting at the same time, "do you have a last name?"

Cora had to swallow to get rid of the dryness in her throat before answering. "It's Walters."

"Cora Walters," Mason murmured, a smile playing across his lips. "Do you have any family?"

Cora looked away. "Not that I know of."

There were a few seconds of silence before Mason spoke again.

"Both of my parents died in a plane crash when I was twelve," he said soberly. "I went to live with my uncle after that. It was difficult, but I was glad that I at least had somebody."

Cora glanced over at him and saw pain and tenderness in his eyes.

"It is hard to be alone," Cora said, a little shocked that she was letting her guard down so easily.

"Maybe I can change that."

A tingle ran through Cora's body, and her mind raced through scenarios that she had always believed would be impossible. But then reality edged back into her subconscious and she shook her head.

"I'm not sure you want to go there," she said bitterly.

"Why not?"

Cora flicked her purple tail. "My situation is complex."

Mason made an effort to flick his metal foot. "So is mine."

Cora laughed in spite of herself, and Mason beamed at her reaction. He took her hand in his.

"Cora, I know what it's like to be different, but I can't even begin to understand what you've been through. You can't imagine how desperately I want to know about you. Please, tell me about your life."

And so, she did. She started with the orphanage and then told him all she could remember about Mrs. Carnivera and the operations. She told him about finding herself trapped in the lagoon with a tail in the place of her legs. She told him what it was like to live with the other mermaids, to sleep in the water, to swim with fish and to communicate with dolphins. She told him things she'd never told anyone else.

When she finished talking, Mason was silent for a long time. At first Cora thought she had freaked him out, but when she looked at his face, his eyes were glistening.

"So, I gather you hate being a mermaid," he said softly.

"Was it obvious enough?" Cora replied with a small smile.

Mason nodded slowly as if he were considering what to say next. "Would you like to see if it can be reversed?"

"Reversed?" Cora repeated, wondering if she'd heard him correctly.

Mason shrugged. "Sure. You weren't born this way. This has been done to you. It can probably be undone."

Cora blinked. She'd never considered it that way. She'd always thought being a mermaid was her fate, that she'd have to live with it forever.

"But, how...?"

Mason held up his hand. "I happen to know someone who dealt quite a bit with situations like this. His name is Doctor Glasser. He's a retired military scientist, and he spent many years experimenting with methods that would allow soldiers to be more effective in the air... and in the water."

Cora stared at him as she let that statement sink in. "You mean, you'd introduce me to this man, and then what? He'd study me?"

Mason chuckled. "There's really not a more delicate way to put it, is there? It would all be very private, but if you're desperate to get out of this lagoon, he would be the one who could help you."

Cora chewed on her lip. If there was any way she could live a fraction of a normal life, she'd take it, even if she had to live without legs. If there was nothing this man could do, then she'd just go back to the lagoon. She really didn't have much to lose.

Cora looked at Mason and smiled. "When can I meet him?"

Chapter Thirteen

Jack was on the verge of quitting his job. He had come in that afternoon and immediately had to grapple with John Olsen, who had somehow made it past the guards at the entrance and was trying to find the mermaids. Jack had found the large man at the water's edge, throwing jewelry into the water. Mr. Olsen had fought back when Jack had tried to take him away from the beach, and now Jack had a large bruise on his jaw. Then he had ventured over to that inlet by the cliffs to see if he could find Cora, and he found her. She was having some kind of picnic and getting all cozy with that Mason Harper guy. Jack had only watched them for a few seconds before he couldn't stand it anymore. He had stomped off to the jungle and yelled at some little girls for jumping too high on the trampoline moss. They had run away in tears and he felt bad for scolding them so harshly, but when he tried to go apologize, he couldn't find them anywhere.

He sat down on a tree stump and held his head in his hands. *Why did I ever take this job?* He thought. He knew why. It was because of Cora. *But what kind of person chooses employment just so they can be close to a girl they hardly know like some kind of creep? No wonder she preferred that other guy.*

"Hey Jack."

Jack started as Tink's voice crackled through his earpiece. "What?" He yelled.

"Whoa, somebody's having a bad day."

Jack blew out a breath. "I'm sorry, Tink. You just startled me, and I haven't gotten a lot of sleep..."

"Oh, I see why you're upset," Tink interrupted. "That dark-haired boy just can't stay away. Tough break."

Jack rolled his eyes. Of course Tink knew. She could see everything.

"For what it's worth, I think that guy is... lame," Tink said with a little chuckle.

Jack groaned. "Let's just not talk about it. What do you need me to do?"

"There are a couple young men testing the perimeter at the jungle-forest border."

"Alright, I'll check it out," Jack said as he stood up. He was suddenly grateful for something to do. He needed a distraction from his thoughts.

Jack found the two guys Tink had described as they were trying to climb a tree to get over the fence.

"Hey, what are you doing?" Jack called out as he approached.

The young men hopped down from the tree and faced Jack. They didn't look very sheepish about trying to break the rules. Rather, they looked defiant.

"We're looking for someone," the larger of the two said, coming closer to Jack than he thought was necessary.

"Well, there's no one back there," Jack replied, gesturing at the fence, "just animals and trees."

"Does Lily Thaman work here?"

Jack frowned at the sudden change of question and the gleam of malice in the young man's eyes.

The other boy piped up. "Short girl, long brown hair, moves like a tiger."

Jack nodded. He remembered Slightly saying something about her. "Yeah. She's in the medic's tent by the arena."

The boys shared a sly look and then headed off in the opposite direction.

Jack shook his head at the odd exchange. Maybe he'd tell Tink to keep an eye on those boys. Something about them made him nervous.

Chapter Fourteen

Cora had been skeptical when Mason had arrived at the inlet with a wheelchair and a blanket, but she had to admit that it was going rather well so far. It had taken a bit of effort to get her into the chair in the first place, and she had felt awkward when she kept slipping out of his grasp, although she hadn't minded being so close to him. Now they were slowly making their way through Neverland, with Mason pushing her as well as he could while also trying to manage his crutch.

"Excuse us," he called out as they came to a large group looking at the Weather Tree. The crowd parted so they could pass through. "Thank you so much," Mason said affably, hobbling over the rough ground. "It's like the blind leading the blind here and this terrain isn't very friendly!"

Cora was wearing a shirt Mason had brought and clutching the blanket that concealed her tail. She was afraid that it would snag on something and reveal her bottom half. Finally they reached the elevator that would take them out of Neverland and into London. Cora was practically shaking with excitement as they waited in line to leave. She hadn't been outside of Neverland since she was a very young girl, and she couldn't wait to see the city.

When they reached the front of the line, the elevator doors opened and Jack Baker stepped out. Cora's breath caught in her throat. If there was anyone that would keep her from leaving Neverland, it would be him. His eyes grew wide as he looked at Cora, then at Mason, then back at Cora. He opened his mouth to say something, then shook his head and walked away. Cora released her breath as Mason wheeled her into the elevator. She was excessively grateful that for once Jack Baker had left her alone.

*****

"That is the most glorious tail I have ever seen! Look at the pattern of the scales! Magnificent!"

The only thing that kept Cora from slapping Doctor Glasser in the face was the fact that he might be able to help her. She was also still in a good mood from everything she had seen on the way to Doctor Glasser's facility. She had been amazed at the enormity of London. The buildings were awe-inspiring, the energy was palpable, the people were so interesting, and there were so many of them. She'd gotten used to the sparse population of Neverland, so being in the midst of all the crowds was a little overwhelming.

They had wound though numerous streets until they came to Doctor Glasser's facility, which seemed rather removed from everything else. The Doctor himself appeared nice enough, if not a bit eccentric and tactless. He was tall and thin with large eyes and wispy grey hair that stuck out at odd angles.

"So, is there any way to get it off?" Cora asked. She was beginning to feel uncomfortable with the way the doctor was stroking her fin as she sat on the operating table.

"Off, my dear? Why, if I had something as glorious as your tail, I'd never want to part with it! Don't you agree, Mason?"

Mason had been observing the initial examination while leaning against the wall, but now he straightened and quirked an eyebrow. "It is a beautiful tail," he said, "but I imagine it would make getting around town rather difficult."

"Not if she lived in Venice," Doctor Glasser commented.

Mason inclined his head. "True, but those canals are notoriously filthy."

Doctor Glasser nodded. "Excellent point." He turned back to Cora. "Well, we won't know anything for sure until we do some scans."

He went to the corner of the room and wheeled over a large, clunky contraption that looked like it hadn't been used in decades. He instructed Cora to lie down on the table, then detached a long apparatus from the main machine and positioned it over the top of her tail. The doctor was about to turn it on when he looked abruptly over at Mason.

"Maybe you'd better leave," Doctor Glasser said. "I don't know what I'm going to find under here, and it's best to give the young lady some privacy."

Mason sighed and secured his crutch. "I suppose you're right, but I hate to miss all the fun." He winked at Cora and left the room.

Cora wasn't thrilled to be alone with the doctor, but she was very glad that Mason wouldn't be there to see whatever freakish elements made up her tail. She knew that Mason liked her, but she didn't want all the gory details of her body to challenge those feelings.

Doctor Glasser powered on the machine, then guided the apparatus down the length of her tail. Then he pushed a few buttons and ran the instrument over her entire body all the way up to her neck. Then he pushed a few more buttons and disappeared to the other side of the machine.

"Oh my."

Cora flinched at the doctor's response, almost dreading what he had found. Doctor Glasser laboriously rotated the machine and directed Cora's attention to a small screen that displayed the internal structure of her body.

"Do you notice anything interesting?" Doctor Glasser asked.

Cora's mouth fell open. "I have legs!"

"That you do, my dear! And quite nice ones, it appears."

Cora ignored the inappropriate compliment and instead stared at the image of the two legs encased in her tail. She tried to move them one at a time, but the action seemed strange.

"And look at this!" Doctor Glasser exclaimed, pointing to a tube running down the length of the tail. "You have one of the most highly developed excretion systems I've ever seen! What a marvelous feat of engineering!"

Cora shifted uncomfortably. Talking about one's personal sewage arrangement was nothing to get excited about.

"Your tail is completely synthetic," the doctor continued, "and it's only attached at your waist. It seems to be grafted into your skin there, but we could cut it off and remove the remaining fibers quite easily, leaving only minimal scarring."

"Really?"

"Yes. With the right tools we could make a few snips, slip it off, frame it, and put it on the wall."

Cora frowned. The thought of mounting her tail on the wall was absurd and sickening. "Can you remove it right now?"

"Oh, no dear. I don't have the proper instruments at the moment. And then there's the matter of detaching that tube..."

"But you could do it, right?"

"Of course. I'd just need a few days to gather the tools."

Cora sighed in relief. It was possible. She could be normal. She had legs, so she was human. Although, there were other parts of her that still didn't make sense.

"If my tail is something someone just stuck on my body, then how can I live and breathe in the water?"

"Ah, this is the most fascinating part," Doctor Glasser replied, pointing to her full body scan and enlarging a spot on her neck. "I believe these tiny incisions are meant to replicate gills."

Cora felt the small bumps below her ear. They'd been there for so long that she'd forgotten that they were out of the ordinary.

"But a few cuts are not enough to enable a person to live in the water," he added. "We'd need more sophisticated equipment to know for sure, but I suspect that your genes are enhanced with the DNA of aquatic creatures."

Cora gulped. "Excuse me?"

"Like I said, it's just a hypothesis at this point, but it's likely that your body taking on the characteristics of fish is through absorbing their DNA. I've seen experiments like this before in the military. It would be incredibly useful for them to have soldiers that could swim abnormally fast, breathe underwater, withstand the pressure of extreme depths, and feel the approach of enemy ships. However, those experiments were never particularly successful. Perhaps the method of your implementation was more advanced."

Cora took a deep breath, trying to process what the doctor had just said. "Will these... characteristics ever go away?"

"I don't see why they would," Doctor Glasser responded with a wide smile. "You'll probably have these skills for the rest of your life."

Cora nodded. So she'd always be abnormal, but at least she could get rid of the most obvious part. "If I come back in a few days, would you remove my tail?"

"If that's what you want, I'd be happy to."

"Thank you," Cora said, already feeling a huge weight being lifted from her shoulders. "I'll find a way to pay you."

The doctor waved his hand dismissively. "Don't worry about it, my dear. Just come back in a week and I'll take care of everything."

*****

"It's been quite a day, hasn't it?" Mason remarked as he helped Cora out of the wheelchair and back into the lagoon by the inlet.

Cora met Mason's eyes and her heart began to pound in her chest. He was kneeling on the ground and he still had his arms around her. "It's been incredible," she replied, trying to keep her voice steady. "Life changing, actually."

She had told Mason what Doctor Glasser had discovered on the way back to Neverland, leaving out some of the more intricate parts, like how she relieved herself and how her genes were probably injected with fish DNA. She had arranged for Mason to take her back the next week so she could have her tail removed.

"So, are you excited to leave this lagoon?" Mason asked, bending down so that his face was even closer to hers.

"More than you could imagine."

Mason smiled. "Well, Cora, you should know that with or without your tail, you are lovely." And then he pressed his fingers against the back of her neck and kissed her. Cora felt like she could melt right there in the water, but she forced herself to hold her ground as she returned his kiss. She said a reluctant goodbye and could still imagine the feel of his lips long after he had disappeared into the jungle.

Chapter Fifteen

Lily restocked the supplies that Slightly had brought her that evening and prepared to close up the medic's tent. She had loved working and living in Neverland for the past few days. Usually she only bandaged up people's minor cuts, but it was far more fulfilling than cleaning rooms at the hospital.

Lily completed her checklist and then stepped out and secured the lock on the canvas door. It was already getting dark and sometimes it was difficult to see as she made her way through the forest to the tiny cabin Slightly had built for her. She had told him she'd be fine sleeping in the underground treehouse with the other boys, but Slightly had insisted that it wouldn't be respectable.

Lily walked through a row of trees and saw her cabin come into view. She took a few more steps and then halted. Something was off. There was too much energy in the air. As her eyes adjusted, she could see the outlines of five boys standing in front of her cabin. She could recognize those boys anywhere. They haunted her dreams.

"Hey Tiger, we found your hideout," said Drake, the oldest of the group.

Lily tensed as her former gang members closed in around her. They were poised to fight and almost all of them had knives. She knew she'd have to act fast if she wanted to stay alive. One of them lunged at her, so she crouched down and swung her leg around, knocking him off his feet. She jumped back up and took advantage of the break in their line, running past them and heading towards the jungle.

She was fast and she knew her way through the trees, but they were gaining on her. She heard someone breathing heavily right behind her. He dove for her and grabbed her ankle, causing her to fall forward. She braced for the impact, but the ground absorbed her. She was encased for a few moments, and then she shot back up into the air. She had fallen on the trampoline moss.

Lily heard shouts of surprise and saw that two of the gang members were also in the moss. She spun around and kicked one while they were in the air, sending him sailing into a zebra tree. She fell down into the moss again, and the other boy punched her in the shoulder as she shot up, but she used the momentum to propel herself over the next patch of moss. She continued to jump from patch to patch until she reached the end of the moss and rolled into a thicket of rum berry bushes. Ignoring the thorns and branches, she crawled into the most dense part of the bushes and waited, hoping she was concealed well enough. A few seconds later, she heard her pursuers run by. She counted to three, then got to her feet and ran towards the cliffs.

Lily remembered there was a cove behind one of the waterfalls that she thought would make a good hiding place. She hoped to be able to hide there until morning, but then she'd have to leave Neverland. The thought filled her with sadness. She had loved working there, and she especially didn't want to leave Slightly, but she couldn't put them all in danger by staying.

She was momentarily distracted by thoughts of Slightly, and she didn't notice that someone was coming at her from the left until he had already jumped on her and pinned her to the ground.

"This is where it ends, Tiger," Drake whispered, smiling triumphantly down at her.

Lily struggled against him, but he held her fast. "You don't have to do this! You're not murderers!"

Drake laughed. "But if we let you get away with what you did, no one will take us seriously."

Lily groaned. "The police will take you *very* seriously. Murder is far more offensive than petty theft."

"They'll have to catch us first."

Lily heard footsteps coming closer as the rest of the gang converged on them and assisted Drake in holding her down. Drake pulled out his knife and held it to her throat.

"Sorry Tiger, but we've got to protect our reputation."

At that moment, a deafening screech ripped through the air. Drake drew his knife back, but the gang still kept their hold on Lily. The ground shook as a monstrous creature came into view. Lily recognized it as the Buffalostrich Rex, but she'd never seen him act so angry before. He was rearing back and snapping his massive jaws. It was dark, but Lily thought she saw Slightly riding on the animal's back.

At the sight of it, the gang released Lily and scattered in fear. The Buffalostrich Rex roared in anger, stomping around and nearly trampling a few of the boys. The creature stooped down and caught Drake's jacket in its teeth, lifting him up and throwing him several meters out of its path. The Buffalostrich Rex then corralled the boys and chased them back through the jungle.

Lily sat up and took deep breaths, trying to process what had just happened. She looked down and saw she had a large gash on her leg, probably from one of the boys' knives.

A few minutes later the Buffalostrich Rex came trotting back towards her. She tensed, but the animal was much more docile this time. The creature stopped in front of Lily, and Slightly slid down from its back and ran towards her.

"Lily! Are you alright? Oh! You're bleeding!" Slightly ripped off a piece of his shirt and wrapped it around Lily's calf. "I learned this from watching a very skilled medic," he remarked, a little playfulness evident in his stressed tone. He ran his hands over Lily's arms and face, checking for more injuries.

Lily finally found her voice. "Slightly, How did you...?" She trailed off, not sure how to express what she had seen.

Slightly sat down next to her. "Tink told me there were some intruders over by your cabin, so I went over to check it out and saw them chasing you. I figured they were from your gang, so I went to get Lamar," he explained, gesturing towards the Buffalostrich Rex. "He'll do anything for a cream puff."

Lily swallowed. "So, are they gone?"

"Yes. They couldn't get to the exit fast enough." Slightly looked sideways at her. "I don't think they'll be back."

Lily shook her head. "You can never be sure. I'll have to leave tomorrow. Maybe I should consider leaving the country."

Slightly grabbed her hand. "Please don't leave, Lily. I'm quite positive Lamar scared them so badly that they won't set foot in here again, but even if they do, I will make sure they don't hurt you. You have to believe that Neverland will be the safest place in the world for you."

Lily stared at him and saw the sincerity in his eyes. She suddenly knew that she belonged in Neverland with Slightly, with this boy that would do anything to protect her. She pulled him towards her and gave him something that was long overdue.

At first he stiffened at her kiss, but then he leaned in and wrapped his arms around her. When she pulled away, he looked back at her in amazement.

"Wow," he exclaimed. "That was way better than I imagined it would be."

Lily laughed and kissed him again until the Buffalostrich Rex nuzzled its furry head between them. With Slightly holding her and a creature with massive teeth just inches from her face, she'd never felt more safe.

Chapter Sixteen

Jack stood at the edge of the lagoon with a forever breathe mask in his hand, wondering whether or not to swim down to the bottom of it. He had decided he was going to quit the next day, which would make this his last night. He still loved Neverland, but these developments with Cora and Mason were just too irritating. He hadn't seen them kiss, and he was glad for that, because the image of it would probably give him an ulcer, but he had heard Tink talking about it, and that, coupled with the fact that Cora had left Neverland with Mason, had made Jack angry enough to want to leave his job.

So now he looked out at the water in a state of indecision. He wanted to see Cora one more time to say goodbye, and maybe tell her how he felt. It was unlikely that he would see her at the surface, so his only option was to go down to her, but he couldn't imagine that she'd be too thrilled about being woken up in the middle of the night just so he could be sentimental. *Well*, he thought, *she already hates me, so I don't have much to lose.* Plus, he'd never have an opportunity like this again. He put on his forever breathe mask and dove into the lagoon.

The water was oddly comforting as it enveloped him. He'd always felt at home in the water, and the mask made swimming even more effortless. He swam down until he found Cora's sleeping pod. He grabbed the side of it to anchor himself and peered in. Cora looked almost blissful as she slept, with a smile tugging at the corner of her lips. Jack suddenly realized what a terrible idea this was, but as he was preparing to turn around, Cora's eyes flew open and she sat up so quickly that she banged her head on the top of her pod. When she focused on Jack, her expression became furious, which was no less than he expected.

He tried to make signs that he wanted to talk to her, but the more she glared at him, the more foolish he felt. Finally she opened her pod and swam out, gesturing for him to follow her. He swam behind her a few meters until they came to something large and spherical. She opened a gate and took him through a tunnel until they emerged into a room with mirrors and gel stools that was only halfway filled with water. She turned on a low light then spun around to face him.

"You'd better have a really good reason for nearly giving me a heart attack!" She exclaimed.

Jack removed his forever breathe mask and rubbed his wet beard. When she put it like that it made him feel like a real jerk. He thought about making up some emergency, but decided against it. He had learned that honesty was always the best option.

"I'm sorry I scared you," he said softly. "I came down to say goodbye."

"Goodbye?" Cora yelled, her face reddening with rage. "You woke me up for goodbye?"

"Yes!" Jack yelled back, feeling a spark of indignation. "I took this job because of you, and now I'm quitting because of you!"

Cora made a face. "Well, that was a dumb thing to do."

"Yes, I've realized that now."

Cora scowled. "What, did you come here to research me? Have I satiated your curiosity? Have you found out everything you need to solve the mystery of the freaky fish girl?"

Jack shook his head in amazement. "No!" he exclaimed, "I came to work here because I like you!"

Cora looked directly into his eyes and softened for a moment, but then she turned away. "Well, in case you hadn't noticed, I have a tail."

"In case *you* hadn't noticed, I don't care!"

"I don't know if that's really sweet or really twisted."

"Neither do I, but it's true, and it's driving me crazy."

Cora rolled her eyes. "Well, let me put you out of your misery."

Jack sighed. "I didn't mean it like that." He ran his hand through his hair. "Look, I know you're not interested. I know you're involved with that Mason guy." He looked down and fiddled with his mask. He didn't really know what to say. He glanced back up at Cora and realized how much he still cared about her. "Just... be careful," he said finally. "Don't trust that guy with everything, you hardly know him."

Cora laughed. "Oh, and I know you so much better?"

Jack shrugged. "We've had some moments."

Cora shifted uncomfortably. "Mason understands me."

Now it was Jack's turn to roll his eyes. "Oh sure. You took one look at him and told him all your secrets."

"It's more than that," Cora shot back defensively.

"It's okay, I get it," Jack said, holding his hands up in defeat. "You like him more than me." Cora raised an eyebrow and Jack added, "A *lot* more than me."

"We have a lot in common."

"Yeah, you're both too attractive for your own good."

Cora gave him a sad smile. It might have been the nicest expression she'd given him in all of their interactions. "I'm sorry, Jack, you seem like a great guy, but I'm just really... complicated."

"I've noticed," Jack replied. He gestured to her tail. "And it's not just because of that."

Cora inclined her head, but she didn't say anything else.

Jack recognized that this was the end of their conversation. "It's been really nice knowing you, Cora. I apologize for waking you up. Good night, and goodbye."

She looked like she might say something, but Jack had had enough for one night. He slipped on his mask and then dove down through the tunnel and out the gate. He passed several exotic fish and a huge sea turtle as he swam back to the surface of the lagoon, but he ignored all of them. He just wanted to get out and forget Neverland forever.

Chapter Seventeen

Peter was in the middle of giving a flying lesson to the boys from Mrs. Nancy's when Slightly rushed into the flying chamber.

"Come with me right now!" He exclaimed, then ran out before Peter could ask for an explanation. He looked around at the roomful of floating boys.

"Hey Trevor, how about you take over?"

The red-haired boy next to him nearly fell to the floor. "Really?"

"Sure. You've been flying for a week now. You're practically a professional."

"Okay!" Trevor said excitedly, giving Peter a toothy grin and flying to the center of the chamber.

Peter exited the chamber and tried to track down where Slightly was. He spotted him running through the jungle towards the beach. He followed after Slightly until he reached the lagoon, where a chaotic crowd was gathered. Peter looked around in confusion. People were yelling at Slightly and Smee, and a few children were even crying.

"We came here specifically to see the show!" A large woman shouted at Slightly. "I demand a refund!"

"You will certainly get one," Slightly replied as calmly as he could. "Just give us a minute to work everything out."

Peter walked over to Slightly. "What's going on?"

"We're still not sure," Slightly said, his voice ragged. "But none of the mermaids showed up for their performance."

Peter raised his eyebrows. "That's strange. I thought they loved doing this show."

"So did I. Maybe they've changed their minds." Slightly rubbed his forehead as another irate visitor approached him. "Could you call Tink and have her check the underwater cameras?"

"Sure." Peter pulled out his two-way radio and paged Tink.

"Hey Peter, what's up?"

"We we wondering if you had eyes on the mermaids."

"I will in a minute," Tink responded. "All of the lagoon cameras went out last night and they're almost done rebooting."

"They went out?"

"Yeah. It happens pretty often, actually. Something about the pressure makes them temperamental."

Peter took a deep breath. He hoped it was just a coincidence, but he had a feeling this was more than just reluctant mermaids and faulty equipment. He waited for a few seconds until Tink's voice crackled through his radio again.

"Okay, the cameras are back up," she said. "And it looks like..."

She was silent for a long time.

"Tink?"

"Peter, the mermaids are gone."

*****

Peter had never seen so many people in central control at once. Curly was there with Tink, Slightly was pacing the small room, and a groggy looking Jack Baker sat in the corner with his head in his hands. Slightly had called him in since he was on duty last night. It almost could have been a party if the mood wasn't so serious.

"So, Jack, where are the mermaids?" Slightly asked.

Jack's head shot up. "How am I supposed to know?"

"Because you were down in the lagoon last night," Tink remarked, pulling up footage of Jack and Cora on one of the screens.

"What were you doing down there?" Peter asked.

"I was saying goodbye," Jack mumbled.

Peter was utterly puzzled. "Why?"

Jack blew out a breath. "Because I like Cora," he admitted in an exasperated tone. "I might even love her. There, I said it. I'm in love with a mermaid. But that doesn't matter, because she's in love with someone else."

They all stared at Jack until Tink spoke up. "So, in a jealous rage you kidnapped her and all of her friends."

Jack threw his hands in the air. "Are you serious? Do you honestly think I would do that?"

"Well, the lagoon cameras went out right after your conversation with Cora," Slightly said. "It does seem a bit suspicious."

"Oh, yes, I carted them all back to my apartment," Jack said sarcastically. "They were a bit disappointed about the size of the bathtub, but I think they'll manage."

Curly snickered. "He does have a point."

"Thank you!" Jack exclaimed. "What would I do with a bunch of mermaids? The idea is absolutely ludicrous!"

"Well, you *were* in a mental institution for a week," Tink countered.

Jack looked like he was about to explode. He ran his hand through his thick hair and took a deep breath. "Do you have footage from the desert last night?"

"Yes," Tink answered, typing in a few commands and scrolling through the footage until Jack came into view.

"I couldn't have kidnapped the mermaids because I was there for the rest of the night," Jack grumbled.

They all leaned forward to look at the screen.

"Jack, were you... building sandcastles?" Slightly asked.

"I was frustrated!" Jack exclaimed. "I needed a distraction! I may be pathetic, but I'm not crazy."

"Maybe if you had been doing your job, the mermaids wouldn't be gone," Slightly snapped.

"Maybe you should fire me," Jack retorted. "It would save me the trouble of having to quit."

"You were going to quit?"

"Yeah. I was going to tell you tonight."

Slightly looked hurt. "Do you not like working here? Is it the pay?"

Peter held up his hand. "Can we get back to the mermaids?"

"Good idea," Tink concurred. "Even if Jack had been doing his job, I don't think he could have prevented this. I've been going through all the feeds, and there's no evidence of anyone going in or out last night."

"How can that be?" Slightly asked. "They couldn't have gone through the lagoon."

Peter groaned. "Yes, they could have." Everyone looked over at him, so he continued. "We drilled a tunnel out of the chambers on the west side of the lagoon to remove the rest of the Liverwood Bank treasure. We were going to fill the tunnel back in, but we've been so busy. We left a temporary seal on the tunnel that's pretty easy to break through."

Slightly nodded somberly. "Okay, so it was someone who knew about the treasure chamber." He paced for a few moments and then turned to Tink. "Didn't you say you found a file about the mermaids the other day?"

"That's right," Tink replied, rolling her chair over to a different screen and pulling up the file. "It looks like the Crocodile was planning on selling information about the mermaids to this guy."

A picture of an older man with a thin face and sparse grey hair filled the screen.

"It says his name is Robert Barlow and he used to work for the military," Tink reported.

"Is there an address?" Peter asked. "Anything that could help us locate him?"

"Not really," Tink said, chewing her lip and clicking through the other documents in the file. "Oh, but it looks like he has a nephew."

She pulled up a photo and everyone except Peter gasped.

"What?" Asked Peter, looking at the young man on the screen. "Who is that?"

"That's Mason Harper," Jacked growled.

Chapter Eighteen

Cora woke to see Mason's face hovering above hers. At first she thought she was dreaming, but something was off. Mason's generally cheerful smile was twisted into an ugly sneer, and she felt cold all over. Something stung her arm and she closed her eyes.

When she woke again, she heard whimpering. She stiffened as she realized that she wasn't in her pod, she wasn't in the lagoon. Her eyes focused on a large, sterile room. She was in Doctor Glasser's facility. She turned her head and saw Isla strapped to an operating table, her eyes wide with fear. Cora looked to the other side. Nerissa, Piper, Meredith and Catalina were all unconscious and bound to operating tables.

How did we get here? Cora thought with growing panic. For a moment she was hopeful that Doctor Glasser was just going to remove her tail earlier than they had planned, but why would all the other mermaids be there? She struggled against her own bonds, but they were unyielding.

"Cora?" Isla whispered, her voice trembling with fear. "What's going on?"

Just then a door opened and Mason walked in. Isla lifted her head and smiled with excitement.

"Mason! I'm so happy to see you! You must be here to save us!"

Isla looked relieved, but Cora narrowed her eyes. He didn't look like he was there to help them. He was carrying a tray of surgical instruments that he set on a small table at the front of the room.

"The fish girls awake," he said, snickering to himself. He glanced over at them with an almost evil smile. He seemed like a completely different person, but it wasn't just his expression that had changed.

"What happened to your foot?" Cora asked through gritted teeth.

Mason laughed, lifting a perfectly normal leg where the metal boot used to be. "That was one of my more brilliant ideas," he boasted. "I figured if I made myself more vulnerable, it'd be easier for you to trust me." He strode over and leered down at her. "And you ate it right up."

Cora tried to lunge at him, but her restraints held her to the table.

Mason smirked and walked to a corner where his crutch was resting. "This little gadget served its purpose as well," he remarked, "although it was horribly cumbersome." He pulled the crutch apart and held up a small camera. "This lovely device was able to record you swimming to the bottom of the lagoon and got all of your tragic secrets, which is very useful evidence."

Cora shook her head. "Why are you doing this?"

Mason set the camera on the table and turned to face her. "I'll let the doctor fill you in on all the gory details, but here's the general idea. You, Cora, and your cohorts here, are extremely valuable."

"To who? The military?"

Mason shrugged. "The military might pay a few thousand, but there are some other corporations that are willing to pay ridiculous amounts of money to find out how to make someone like you." He walked forward and stroked Cora's hair. She jerked her head away from him. "With that kind of money I can finally become the actor I was meant to be. No more dinner theatre, no more children's birthday parties, no more petty cons for my uncle. I can practically pay my way to the big screen!"

Cora glared at him. "I can't believe I actually thought you liked me."

Mason gave her a pitying look. "You are quite a beautiful creature, Cora." Then his face morphed into one of disgust. "But you have gills!"

Cora shook with anger. "Well, *you're* the one who kissed me!"

He raised an eyebrow. "Believe me, I've kissed far more repulsive girls for money."

Cora thrashed her tail so hard that her operating table nearly tipped over. Mason looked nonplussed and turned away.

"No more hiding, Cora," he said, picking up a syringe from the tray. "You're going to be famous. Although, you won't be able to enjoy the spotlight, because you'll probably be dead."

"Why?" Isla squeaked, her face pale with fear. She had been so quiet, Cora had forgotten she was awake.

Mason sauntered over to Isla and leaned casually on her operating table. "Because we're going to dissect all of you."

"No!" Isla cried, her body shaking uncontrollably.

"But first I have to sedate you again," Mason said, holding the syringe to Isla's arm. The young girl tried to resist, but she was so scared that she didn't put up much of a fight. Mason injected her with the sedative and her eyes rolled back into her head. Her golden tail flinched twice, and then she was still.

Mason retrieved another syringe from the tray and came towards Cora. "You're a lot stronger than I thought," he remarked. "Usually two doses of this stuff is enough to knock someone out for days."

Cora clenched her jaw. She knew she didn't stand a chance against him while she was strapped to the table, but she wasn't going to make it easy. He bent down over the crook of her arm and Cora was about to bash her head into his, but suddenly the door burst open and Mason sprang away from her. Cora looked over and saw something she never imagined would make her heart soar.

Standing in the doorway was the glorious sight of Jack Baker.

Chapter Nineteen

"Who are you?" Mason asked with a sneer.

In reply, Jack stepped up to Mason and punched him in the face.

"Ah! I think you broke my nose!" Mason screeched, hunching over in pain. "Do you have any idea how much my face is worth?"

"I'd say it's worth a few good laughs," Jack said, walking towards Cora.

"What are you doing?"

"I'm going to take these ladies off your hands."

Mason laughed. "Is that so? Are you going to tie them together and drag them out of here?"

"No, I brought help."

Mason glanced at the door and then back at Jack. "You're lying."

"Maybe, but how much are you willing to gamble? There's plenty more I could do to mess up your face."

Cora watched as they stared at one another. Now that she saw them together, she realized how superior Jack was. He was taller and more muscular. And while Mason had a handsome face, his features seemed weak compared to Jack's. And there was the fact that Mason had turned out to be a slimy dirtbag. That lessened his appeal considerably. Their standoff was interrupted by Doctor Glasser rushing into the room with a gun.

"Don't move!" He shouted, his hands shaking as he aimed the gun at Jack.

"Are you sure you want to shoot me, Doctor Barlow?" Jack said evenly. "I don't think you want to add homicide to your long list of criminal offenses."

The doctor blanched. "How do you know that? How do you know my name?"

"We did our research," Jack replied, taking a step forward. "With an extremely talented hacker, it didn't take long to discover that Steven Glasser was in fact Robert Barlow, who had a history of selling military secrets and running cons with his nephew, Mason Barlow."

"You couldn't possibly have evidence on me," Mason said haughtily.

"On the contrary, the Ladies Biscuit Club of Brenton is quite irate about the handsome young caterer that took off with the profits from their spring bazaar."

Mason reddened and took a swing at Jack, which he dodged easily. Mason's forward momentum caused him to stumble into the table Meredith was lying on. She jerked awake and looked around. Her eyes settled on Jack.

"Oh yeah. That beard is hot," she said groggily, then fell back unconscious on the table.

They all stared at Meredith for a moment, and then Jack made a lunge for the gun in Doctor Barlow's hand. He grabbed the doctor's arm, but the older man spun out of his grip and Jack fell to the floor next to Cora. He pulled himself up by grabbing the side of her table, and Cora flinched as she felt something cold against her wrist. She glanced down and saw Jack quickly cutting the strap holding her arm, then he pressed the knife into her hand before he ran at Doctor Barlow again. Mason tripped him and Jack fell to the floor again, but he swung his leg around to knock Mason off of his feet. Cora used the commotion to cut through the straps on her tail, but soon everyone was on their feet again.

"Would you shoot him already!" Mason yelled at his uncle.

"Go ahead," Jack said. "But the police will be here soon."

"Even if that's true, the dissections will only take a few minutes and then we can get out of here."

Jack's face filled with rage. "Dissections?" He exclaimed. "You guys are barbaric."

"Oh please," Doctor Barlow scoffed. "They're only half human."

Jacked growled and charged at the doctor, lowering his shoulder into the older man's midsection and sending him flying into the wall. The gun clattered to the floor and Mason dove for it before Jack had a chance to get it.

"Ha!" Mason exclaimed, standing at the foot of Cora's operating table and aiming the gun at Jack. "You'll find I'm not as hesitant to shoot as my uncle."

Cora flicked her tail. Jack caught her eye and chuckled. "I would be careful, Mason. You're standing in a very dangerous place."

Mason turned around just in time for Cora to slap him in the face with her tail.

"Argh!" Mason screamed, stumbling backwards. "Would you people leave my face alone!"

"You're right," Jack remarked. "We wouldn't want you to look bad for your mug shot."

As if on cue, the door flew open and Slightly rushed in, followed by a dozen armed officers. Mason dropped the gun and Doctor Barlow put his hands up. The officers handcuffed the pair and led them out of the room, and Mason whined the whole way. Cora couldn't help but think of how pathetic Mason had turned out to be. How could she have been so stupid?

An officer who seemed to be in charge turned to Jack. "Good work, Baker," he said, slapping him heartily on the shoulder. "You know you've got a job if you ever decide to come back."

"I'll let you know if I change my mind," he replied.

The officer nodded and followed the others out.

"That was close," Slightly said, blowing out a breath. "I'm glad we got here in time."

"Me too." Jack said.

"But Tink sending that evidence straight to the station's database really sped up the process. Thanks for the tip."

Jack shrugged. "When you work with the police, you learn all sorts of shortcuts." Jack walked to the table in the front of the room and picked up the small camera from

Mason's crutch. "This will need to be destroyed," he said, handing it to Slightly. "And do you think you could take a look around and collect any other information they might have gathered on these girls?"

"Sure," Slightly responded. He glanced at Cora and gave Jack a meaningful look, then left the room.

Jack sighed and turned to face Cora. Her breath caught in her throat for a minute as she took in the sight of him. She wished that it hadn't taken being kidnapped and almost killed by a psychopath for her to realize just how incredible he was. He approached her and picked up the knife she had left on her operating table. He easily cut through the rest of her straps, but then he winced and stepped back apologetically.

"I'm sorry, I should have asked first," he said, looking a bit sheepish.

Cora quirked an eyebrow and quickly sat up. She grabbed his shirt and pulled him to her until her lips were on his. After a few seconds she pulled away and smiled.

"I'm sorry, I should have asked first," she said playfully.

Jack's hazel eyes were gleaming as he looked at her. "Believe me, there's no need." Then he sat down on the table and pulled her into his lap, tail and all, and kissed her until all of the horrors of the past few hours faded away.

Chapter Twenty

"Alright ladies, everyone look at the camera," the reporter called out to the mermaids. "Ready? One, two... actually, let's put the short one in the center."

Nerissa gasped. "What? But I'm always in the middle!"

"Sorry. That one's a better focal point."

Isla blushed as she moved to the center of the group, while Nerissa gave her a murderous look.

"Okay. One, two, smile!" The reporter snapped the photo and the mermaids moved out of their formation. Peter watched Meredith take a couple steps forward and promptly fall to the ground.

"Ugh. Walking is hard!" She complained.

The reporter frowned. "What does she mean by that?"

Cora, who had been watching off the to the side, quickly stepped over. "She just means that sometimes they tire their legs out so much in the water that it's difficult to walk."

The reporter seemed satisfied, and Peter and Slightly shared a look of relief.

The past couple weeks had been interesting as the mermaids transitioned out of their tails. After the kidnapping, they had decided that for the mermaids' safety, they should all have their tails removed. Lily had done some research and was ultimately able to perform the operation herself, which allowed them to take care of the issue privately. Slightly had designed some temporary mermaid tails for them to put on for the show, but the rest of the time they usually went around on their legs, which had taken some adjusting. They spent a lot of the day walking around Neverland and sometimes London, but all of them were still living in the lagoon. Except for Cora.

Cora had been acting as the mermaids' spokesperson for the past couple weeks, which was especially helpful since Slightly had finally agreed to allow some of the news outlets to have short interviews with the Neverland mermaids and photograph them. She had moved into an apartment in London and was spending a lot of time with Jack Baker, but in a few months she would travel to Mexico, where she had been recruited by a specialized team to help research dolphins.

Peter smiled as he watched Jack and Cora holding hands on the beach, and he suddenly wished that Wendy were there. He decided he'd visit her after he'd finished the morning's business.

"Okay, that's all we have time for," Slightly told the reporter, ushering him away from the mermaids. "We've got to get ready to open the park."

The reporter reluctantly packed his things and Slightly walked over to Peter.

"Hey, we've got that big birthday party today," Slightly said. "Are you going to go pick up the food?"

"I'm going right now," Peter assured him. "Hey Nibs," he called out, "could I get your help picking up some food from the bakery?"

Nibs, who had been whittling a stick with his knife, jumped up. "Sure, if you need help."

Peter smiled. He didn't really need help, he just wanted to bother Susan by bringing Nibs along. They went up the lift into London and walked several blocks to the bakery. It was early morning and there was a thick fog that obscured everything over three meters tall.

"What is *he* doing here," Susan exclaimed when they walked into the bakery.

"He's helping me pick up the sandwiches," Peter said innocently. "Are they ready?"

Susan gave Nibs a nasty glare and then disappeared into the kitchen. She came back with a few trays and set them on the counter. Peter filled out a form and paid for the food, then stacked the trays and lifted them up.

Nibs had been examining the pastries and he walked up to the counter. "Could I get one of those cherry jelly doughnuts, please."

Susan raised her eyebrows. "Cherry? Are you sure?"

Nibs looked a bit confused. "Yes, cherry."

Susan crossed her arms. "It's just that not everybody likes cherry."

"I do. It's my favorite flavor."

Susan leaned forward. "Are you sure you wouldn't like that chocolate cake over there?"

Nibs glanced at the cake and shook his head. "What would I do with a cake? I'll just take the cherry doughnut, please. That's all I want."

A slow smile spread across Susan's face as she retrieved the doughnut and handed it to him. "You know, Nibs, the last time we spoke, I believe I forgot to give you my number."

Nibs stared at her. "I didn't ask for it."

"Well, you should have."

Several minutes later, after Susan had sufficiently affected Nibs with her powers of flirtation, they emerged from the bakery with the trays of food.

"Nibs, do you think you could take these down to Neverland?" Peter asked. "I'm going to stop by Wendy's house."

"Sure, whatever you need," Nibs replied, seeming a bit dazed as he took the sandwiches from Peter and headed down the street.

Peter glanced up at the fog that stretched like a blanket above him. *With this kind of cover, no one would see me flying,* he thought with a mischievous grin. Glad that he was wearing his flying suit under his clothes, he shed his outer layers and rubbed some pixie dust on himself. He ran towards a large building until he felt the opposing forces, then twisted and took off into the air.

Rising above the fog, he wove in and out of the spires and structures that were poking through the heavy mist. He arrived at Wendy's building and hovered at her window, tapping on the glass until she noticed him.

"Peter!" Wendy exclaimed, opening the window and pulling him inside. He was still floating as she reached up to kiss him. He wrapped his arms around her and pulled her to him so that her weight brought him down to the floor.

"We do have a door, you know."

Peter and Wendy quickly pulled apart at the sound of Mrs. Darling's voice. She was standing against the wall, looking at them with an expression that was halfway between amusement and worry.

"I apologize, Mrs. Darling," Peter said. "It's quicker this way."

Mrs. Darling waved her hand. "Peter, how many times do I have to tell you to just call me Angela?"

"Of course. Sorry, Mrs. Darling." Peter replied with a wink.

Wendy laughed and took Peter's hand. "He's just trying to be respectful, mom."

Mrs. Darling raised an eyebrow. "I'm not sure I believe that." She sat on the edge of Wendy's bed. "So, how is everything in Neverland?"

"It's great," Peter said. "Have you gotten a chance to come yet?"

Mrs. Darling nodded. "I've been twice now, and it looks fantastic." A sadness settled over her features. "Although, it seems a bit of the magic is missing."

Peter smiled. "You can find that magic during visiting hours at Belmarsh Prison."

At first Mrs. Darling looked scandalized, but then she inclined her head. "I suppose I could."

"I know the captain would love to see you."

"Perhaps." Mrs. Darling stared at the wall for a few moments and then stood up. "Well, I'll let you two get back to your innocent and very controlled kissing," she said with a meaningful look. Wendy blushed as Mrs. Darling headed out of the room, but still gave Peter a long kiss as soon as her mother was gone.

"What brings you here this morning?" She asked him.

It took a few moments for Peter to clear his head enough to answer her. "I was wondering if you'd like to fly to Neverland."

Wendy's eyes lit up. "I'd love to." She quickly went to change into her flying suit and apply some pixie dust, and then joined him on the window ledge.

Peter looked over at Wendy, remembering how he'd felt the first time he saw her. A lot had happened since then, but he was so glad he had lost his shadow all those months ago.

"Are you ready?" She asked, her blue green eyes shining.

Peter nodded and took her hand. She winked at him, and Peter laughed as together they jumped off the ledge and flew out the window.

Made in the USA
Monee, IL
01 July 2022

98939519R00069